FREEDOM'S
Flight

PENNY ZELLER

Print ISBN: 978-1-957847-02-3

Front cover design by Cynthia Gilbert

Typography and back cover by mountainpeakedits.com/

Editing by mountainpeakedits.com/

This novel is a work of fiction. Unless otherwise indicated, all the names, characters, businesses, places, events, and incidents in this book are either a figment of the author's imagination or used in a fictitious manner. Any resemblance to actual persons, living or dead, is purely coincidental.

All scripture quotations are taken from the King James Version of the Bible.

Standalone Novels

Love in Disguise

Wyoming Sunrise Series

Love's New Beginnings (Prequel)

Forgotten Memories

Dreams of the Heart

Love Letters from Ellis Creek Series

Love from Afar

Love Unforeseen

Love Most Certain

Love in Chokecherry Heights Series

Henry and Evaline (Prequel)

Love Under Construction

Standalone Novellas

Freedom's Flight

Horizon Series

Over the Horizon

Montana Skies Series

McKenzie

Kaydie

Hailee

Nonfiction

77 Ways Your Family Can Make a Difference

Dedicated to the courageous men and women who risked their lives to aid those trapped in slavery to their newfound freedom along the Underground Railroad.

Cast thy burden upon the Lord, and he shall sustain thee: he shall never suffer the righteous to be moved.
~ Psalm 55:22

Chapter One

ANNALISE VAN HOUTEN FOLLOWED her aunt and uncle toward the First Church of Ridge Gap, Tennessee. The stately brick building loomed over an otherwise modest town square.

Yet for all of the church's opulent outer appearance, inside its doors, hypocrisy reigned. Hypocrisy that Annalise wanted no part of.

She cast a glance across the street and up the road. A steeple rose above a humble white church. It reminded her of the church she attended with her parents in Virginia before their deaths.

A place of true worship.

"Come along, Annalise, or we shall be late," Aunt Lavinia rebuked.

At twenty years of age, shouldn't Annalise have a right to choose where she wished to worship?

Not if I am constantly under the control of Aunt Lavinia and Uncle Phineas.

"Aunt Lavinia, might I attend the church just up the road for this time only?"

1

And all the other times until I'm at least ninety-five...

Aunt Lavinia stopped and turned abruptly to face Annalise. Thankfully, Uncle Phineas was discussing with one of the elders the rewards for runaway slaves.

"Surely you jest, Annalise. First Church has always been our church. Why would you desire to go elsewhere?"

Retorts came to Annalise, most of them unacceptable to Aunt Lavinia. Half-truths filled her mind. But she couldn't, wouldn't lie. "I—"

"Are you doing your best to shame our good name by attending a paltry church with no parishioners of high social standing?"

"No, I just...it reminds me of the church I attended with my parents."

"Feeling nostalgic, are you?" Aunt Lavinia narrowed her eyes, but they seemed to soften for one brief moment.

"I promise, Aunt Lavinia, that no one in our social circle will be the wiser as to my choice in where to worship. Nehemiah can deliver me to the front door and retrieve me when it's over."

"What if the church you wish to attend has a longer service? We won't be waiting around for you."

"I would not expect you to, Aunt Lavinia."

"Won't you miss being able to discuss individuals' fashion, or lack thereof, with the other women in the congregation, as we do at our church?"

Not in the least. Besides, they are your friends, not mine. Annalise hadn't been able to make any friends in her new home. She pushed aside the disheartening thought.

"I promise to sit in the back of the church and watch the door for Nehemiah. Have him retrieve me when the services at First Church have concluded, and I will leave posthaste."

"I really should ask your uncle." Aunt Lavinia turned her perfectly-coifed head toward her husband. "On second thought, he is in a deep discussion with Luther Hiram." She lowered her voice and rolled her eyes. "You know how they get when they discuss runaway slaves that have made it all the way to Canada. Phineas becomes a sourpuss for the remainder of the day. Best not to ask him anything if you desire a favorable response."

"I agree. Perhaps this is a situation better handled without him."

Did I really just say that? Annalise rebuked herself for allowing the words to tumble from her mouth.

"I suppose you are right. Run along then."

Ten minutes later, she found herself in the back pew of the Ridge Gap Bible Church. Due to her tardiness, parishioners were already singing hymns when she arrived. The sound of their voices lifted to the Lord filled Annalise's heart, and she merged her voice, singing with devotion to her Savior.

The church was full, almost to capacity. Annalise noted immediately that she stood out among the rest of the women with her elaborate dress. A few glances her way made her feel self-conscious, but she quickly dismissed the thought. Finally, she was in a place where she could fully worship the Lord.

A handsome young man approached the weathered podium and introduced himself as the Reverend Matthias Sorenson. His love for the Lord was evident as he began to preach. What a contrast between the sermons of Ridge Gap Bible Church and First Church!

All was quiet at supper. That was, until Aunt Lavinia decided to speak. Annalise watched her aunt dab at the corners of her mouth with exaggeration. "Annalise, your uncle and I would like to announce a guest who is coming for a visit tomorrow evening."

Annalise inwardly groaned. Aunt Lavinia's "guests" were never a good thing.

"His name is Dale Hiram, and he's the son of an esteemed acquaintance, Luther Hiram." Aunt Lavinia tapped her long nails on the table. "You would do well to make it a point to be gracious and congenial."

Uncle Phineas glowered from across the table. "Not like the immature actions you indulged in with the last fine young gentleman your aunt attempted to introduce to you."

Annalise shivered, even though the house was stifling from the high humidity. Beulah, one of the slaves, did her best to fan the family, but the constant flow did little to reduce the summer heat. The man Aunt Lavinia had attempted to introduce to Annalise last time was far from a young man—at least forty—in Annalise's estimation.

His eyes had traveled up and down her body and his leering expression had caused vomit to rise in her throat.

"Don't be too harsh with her, Phineas. She is young and naïve as to the importance of finding a suitable husband."

"She's twenty-years-old. Hardly a child," growled Uncle Phineas.

"True, and I was embarrassed for days by her actions. The women in our social circle fussed unmercifully." Aunt Lavinia's wide forehead puckered. "It took some time to rectify the situation." She paused and let out a theatrical sigh. "Annalise, please do attempt to appreciate that we only want what is best for you. Or do you intend to be a spinster and reside here in our home upon our merciful act of charity for the remainder of your days?"

Never would I desire such a fate! But Annalise didn't allow the thought to escape her mouth. While she never would have chosen to reside with her aunt and uncle, it was the only home she had, and Annalise didn't wish to suddenly become homeless.

"Move the fan faster, Beulah," snapped Aunt Lavinia. "I declare. If you do not do better than the ghastly job you are doing, we will have no choice but to sell you."

Annalise tossed Beulah a sympathetic glance. The poor woman was doing her best. How her hand did not fall off from the constant motion was beyond Annalise.

Uncle Phineas scowled. "I never wanted her in the first place. We inherited several slaves from your parents when they died, Annalise. We have six of them left in this household. Many were sold because of their refusal to do an adequate job."

"And many of them," quipped Aunt Lavinia, pointing a long, crooked finger at her niece, "had to leave because you became friends with them."

The accusation made Annalise's stomach hurt. She had always thought of the slaves they owned as friends and, while her parents had owned slaves, they treated them well. Of course, Annalise's parents were godly Christian folks. Her aunt and uncle were the opposite. They called themselves Christians, but none of their behavior exhibited such a title. Wealth and power were their only concerns.

After now residing with her relatives and seeing their treatment of fellow human beings, Annalise had come abhor slavery and to not condone it at all.

"Did you hear what I just said, Annalise?"

"Yes, ma'am."

"Good. Then you'll do well enough alone to treat the slaves as they deserve to be treated."

As animals? As less than human? Never.

"You should be grateful we allow you to live here at all. Your father was not on the best of terms with his sister. And I, quite frankly, never cared for the man," sneered Uncle Phineas.

Nor did he care for you, Uncle Phineas.

"True, indeed." Aunt Lavinia again tapped her nails on the table. "Your father and I were never close, and he made his feelings known about his disapproval of my marriage to Phineas. It's only out of the goodness of our hearts that we allow you to live here with all the freedoms most people wish for."

Freedoms? What freedoms? You allow me to live here only to manage the funds left behind by my parents.

Annalise bit her lip. To retort would do no good. She'd tried it once.

That was the day she had realized just how evil her aunt and uncle could be.

That night was the same as many nights at the Thorn household. Annalise's only reprieve from her aunt and uncle's watchful eye was when she turned in for the night. Her small room on the second floor was her sanctuary.

Her lady's maid, Jinny, helped Annalise into her nightdress. That was when the tears began to fall.

Tears over the loss of Annalise's beloved parents. She missed them so! Why had the cholera taken them so soon?

Why hadn't God taken Annalise too?

Such a fate would be far better than what she now had to endure.

Tears over leaving her life in Virginia, only to be brought here to reside with Aunt Lavinia and her horrid husband, Phineas.

Grief over the way the slaves at the Thorn household were treated. Abuse of the slaves was rampant. Beatings, a daily occurrence. Whenever Uncle Phineas tired of any of the slaves, he merely sold them to the highest bidder.

If they survived his wrath.

Annalise's parents had never once sold a slave. They had never once allowed one to be beaten.

Only six of the Van Houten slaves remained—Beulah, Jinny, Tandey, Nehemiah, and two other male slaves in the fields.

Annalise was against slavery. But what could she do?

How could one person make a difference?

And with Aunt Lavinia and Uncle Phineas watching her every move, she had no freedom.

Lord, I beseech Your help, for right now, I feel helpless.

CHAPTER TWO

ANNALISE WALKED DOWN THE boardwalk and past the shops. The freedom of having a few minutes without the presence of Aunt Lavinia's oppressive personality refreshed her. She would certainly take advantage of the brief respite while her aunt was chatting with one of her high society friends.

"Hello, Miss Van Houten." Sheriff Bleyer interrupted Annalise's thoughts.

"Sheriff."

The sheriff swaggered toward Annalise and cornered her. Something about his stance and unrelenting stare left goose pimples on Annalise's arms. He was a man of the law, so surely she was overreacting. "Tell me, Miss Van Houten, how are you takin' to attendin' Ridge Gap Bible Church?"

Was it Annalise's imagination, or was there a note of sarcasm in the sheriff's voice? "It is a Christ-loving church."

"So you enjoy attendin'?"

"I do."

How did the sheriff even know she attended the humble church? As soon as the question popped into her head, Annalise pushed it aside. Of course he knew. Nothing was a secret in Ridge Gap, least of all when Phineas and Lavinia Thorn's niece decided to attend another church.

How scandalous!

"From what I understand, you've been attendin' for the past two weeks now." His never-blinking gimlet-eyed stare unnerved her.

"Sheriff Bleyer, I have every mind to believe you are interrogating me."

The sheriff appeared shocked. "Not at all, ma'am, not at all." He turned and gestured toward the Ridge Gap Bible Church. "I was just wonderin' how you like the place is all."

"I like it fine, Sheriff. Perhaps you should attend sometime." She mimicked him and motioned toward the church.

"No thank you, ma'am. I prefer First Church," he said, a self-righteous gleam in his hardened hazel eyes. "Have a good day."

Annalise watched Sheriff Bleyer strut down the boardwalk. Why had he chosen to intimidate her?

Matthias saw her from his position near the mercantile.

The lovely woman who had attended church services twice now.

But she didn't take any notice of him. Instead, she chatted with Sheriff Bleyer.

The enemy.

Matthias watched the woman point in the direction of the church. Was she discussing something she'd discovered about the church with the sheriff?

Something akin to several members of the church assisting slaves in escaping to freedom?

Worry niggled at him. The last thing they needed was to have their plans exposed. Too many lives were at stake. Matthias thought he had paid close enough attention to the newcomer. Now, he wasn't so sure. Traitors, as he knew full well, didn't all look the same. Cloaked in dishonesty and selfishness, betrayal was second nature to them.

Which was why Matthias couldn't afford to be gullible.

He should have made time to ask her about herself last week. But the parishioners had been overly eager to discuss the sermon afterward, depriving him of the chance.

"Reverend, so nice to see you." Portly Mrs. Knapp bustled her way out of the mercantile and nearly collided with Matthias.

Matthias reluctantly drew his attention from the woman and Sheriff Bleyer. "Hello, Mrs. Knapp. Nice to see you as well." He grunted inwardly at how unconvincing his voice sounded. Not at all fitting for one leading the flock.

"Why, Reverend, if my eyes don't deceive me, I would say you might be captivated by that young lady."

Could Mrs. Knapp speak any louder or be any more obvious? Matthias knew red crept up his freshly-shaven face.

Lovely woman? Yes. Captivated by her? Perhaps. A possible threat? Yes.

Mrs. Knapp glanced from him to the woman, then back to him. While Mrs. Knapp was a dear soul, she quite often partook in gossip. Should she truly believe Matthias was "captivated", word would spread throughout the church—and the town—within a matter of minutes.

"Now, Reverend, there is no shame in being mesmerized by a certain young lady's beauty. Why, when I was a few years younger, my husband—you do know that Basil and I have been married for forty years, don't you?"

"Yes, ma'am." Matthias kept his gaze on the woman, but his attention on Mrs. Knapp.

"Anyhow, when I was a few years younger, long before Basil and I married, Basil was enchanted by my loveliness. I was quite comely and he could scarcely take his eyes from me when we were introduced that fateful day. Now, forty years and four months later, we are still happily joined in matrimony. That could happen to you too, Reverend. Even if that lovely young woman is far above your station."

Far above his station or not, Matthias had no interest in a woman who might endanger the lives of those seeking freedom and those helping them attain it.

That evening, Matthias pushed the food around on his plate. Betsy had done a fine job making the meal, but he just wasn't hungry.

"You're in deep thought," observed Betsy.

"Haven't spoken a word all evening," added her husband, Adam.

"What's on your mind, Matthias?"

Matthias eyed his younger sister. So often he had given thought to what would happen to her if the opposition knew.

He must never allow her to be implicated. He would take complete and utter responsibility before he allowed her to even be accused.

"Did either of you see the woman who has been attending church these past two Sundays and sits in the back pew?"

"The one in the fancy gown?"

"Yes."

"I noticed her too," added Adam. "Never seen her at our church before. What do you reckon she wanted?"

"Perhaps to worship?" teased Betsy.

"Funny, Bets. I'm concerned about why she was there," Matthias said.

"It's a peculiar day when we become concerned why folks attend church." Betsy let out a soft laugh, then continued, her overly-large eyes growing even larger. "I admit I wondered who she was as well. Folks of high society don't usually attend our church. Maybe she meant to attend First Church and became lost."

Matthias thought it unlikely, but he didn't mention so. Always the optimist, his sister would likely think him absurd for even considering the woman's affiliation with the enemy. "Did she appear to be listening to the sermon?"

"Devoutly," answered Betsy. "Matthias, what is this all about?"

"I saw her speaking with Sheriff Bleyer today."

Adam stopped chewing his roast chicken and narrowed his eyes. "She was speaking with Sheriff Bleyer? Did you happen to hear the conversation?"

"No. But I did notice her pointing to the church."

"Oh, Matthias, you are always such a distrustful sort," Betsy declared. "She probably needed directions."

"My concern is that she may have been sent by Sheriff Bleyer, Phineas Thorn, or one of the others to try to find out if we are involved in assisting the slaves to freedom."

Betsy tilted her head to one side. "Because she was merely speaking to Sheriff Bleyer?"

"Bets, I know you try to see the best in others, and I commend you for that. But sometimes we have to be realistic."

Adam nodded. "Especially after nearly losing our lives with Gene's deception."

Adam was the only other one who knew the entire details of their former friend's treachery. Had the Lord not been watching over them, Matthias and Adam would have already been hanged, or at the very least, doing time in their former town's county jail.

"I watched her for a while. Although Mrs. Knapp was doing her best to distract me."

Betsy began to laugh. "That Mrs. Knapp is quite ornery."

"That she is. Of more serious concern, we can't have anything or anyone thwart our plans, and with Sheriff Bleyer nosing around..."

"Oh, Matthias. You're so leery. The woman may have heard that you have wonderful sermons and how you encourage folks to live for our Savior. You do have a reputation here in Ridge Gap."

Matthias knew Betsy was only good-naturedly chiding him. Still, he couldn't let go of his worry.

"Trust, Matthias. Just trust."

"I'm trying, Bets, but it doesn't come easy."

"Cast thy burden upon the LORD, and he shall sustain thee: he shall never suffer the righteous to be moved." The verse from Psalm 55:22 burrowed into his heart.

Now if only his mind could believe it.

Chapter Three

THE FOLLOWING SUNDAY, ANNALISE again attended Ridge Gap Bible Church. After a month of listening to Pastor Sorenson's sermons, she found herself digging deeper into God's Word and full of gratitude that Uncle Phineas and Aunt Lavinia allowed her to continue attending the church.

She had also exchanged pleasantries with some of the other folks at the church. Perhaps they would accept her, even if she was not at all like them. For they had the most important thing in common—Jesus.

Without hesitation, Annalise had become friends with Betsy Woods, Reverend Sorenson's sister.

One afternoon after church services, Annalise wandered outside, waiting for Nehemiah to retrieve her. She scanned the road. Where was he? Of course, with her aunt and uncle deciding not to attend church today, Annalise could have been forgotten.

She returned inside and heard soft voices. A group of people, all men, except Betsy, and including Reverend

Sorenson and Mr. Woods, spoke, their voices barely above a whisper.

"The Faith Train will be leaving again in two days." Reverend Sorenson's voice.

The Faith Train?

"We still need more clothes for the runaways. Betsy, do you have enough fabric to sew three pairs of trousers and three shirts?"

Runaways? As in runaway slaves?

"I do. That's a lot to sew in such little time."

"Perhaps one of the ladies from church could join you in sewing. You could mention that the clothes are for the less fortunate in our community," suggested Reverend Sorenson. "That is the truth," he added.

"Indeed," answered Betsy, "I have just the person in mind. Annalise Van Houten has considerable experience in sewing from her boarding school days. I can tell her it's for the less fortunate, and I am sure she would be willing to assist."

Me?

Annalise sucked in her breath and willed her heart not to pound loudly enough for the others to hear it. *Why would they be speaking of such delicate matters as runaway slaves? Could they not get caught and hanged if someone other than me had crept back into the church?*

"You must be sure not to tell her who will be the true recipients," Reverend Sorenson said. "We don't know if we can trust her. She is Phineas Thorn's niece after all."

Why could you not trust me? Annalise shoved the pang of disappointment aside. *I certainly did not ask to be Uncle Phineas's niece.*

"I'll not divulge the information," answered Betsy.

The conversation among the group continued with vague plans.

Lord, please don't let them hear me.

Annalise tiptoed her way to the door, pushed it open, and stepped into the sunlight once more. Had she really just heard a conversation about runaway slaves?

Nehemiah arrived then, and escorted Annalise into the carriage. Two things were for certain: More than anything, Annalise wanted to be a part of the Faith Train and aid the slaves. And for some reason, she desired Reverend Sorenson to know he could trust her. Even with such a sensitive matter.

"I never imagined I would use the skills I acquired at the boarding school to sew clothing for the less fortunate," said Annalise. She and Betsy had spent the morning stitching trousers and shirts.

Would her new friend someday tell Annalise the truth of who would wear these clothes?

Betsy giggled, interrupting Annalise's ponderings. "Nor had I have imagined that I would be sewing at all, given the fact that I abhorred such a task until I was married and had no other choice."

The "sewing circle" with Betsy was the one place that Aunt Lavinia allowed Annalise to frequent besides church. In Aunt Lavinia's mind, the "sewing circle" furthered Annalise's chances of marriage in the near future by advancing her sewing skills. Annalise would take any opportunity that presented itself to be free of the strict confinement of the Thorn Plantation.

And help the "less fortunate" at the same time.

She hadn't admitted that the sewing circle contained only her and Betsy.

"I am thrilled you accepted my invitation," said Betsy. "It has been most delightful getting to know you through church."

"And you as well." *Not to mention finding out tidbits about your older brother.*

But although Reverend Sorenson was a handsome man who obviously loved the Lord, one thing was clear. He did not trust Annalise or her intentions.

Never had she been more thrilled to be a part of a plan to free those so wrongly held in captivity. Mother and Father would be proud. Annalise prayed long and hard that the Lord Almighty would show her a way to make a difference.

And show her, He had.

A noise interrupted the women's comfortable camaraderie and conversation. Annalise peered out the window at the wagon that had just arrived.

"It appears Matthias and Adam are here for the noonday meal." Betsy placed her stitching on the table.

"May I assist with the preparations?"

"Certainly."

Grateful that Betsy never judged her because of her affluent upbringing and the fact that Annalise had never prepared a meal in her life, Annalise rose to help her friend.

Reverend Sorenson entered the room while Mr. Woods remained in the wagon. "Betsy, Miss Van Houten."

Was it Annalise's imagination or did his startling, warm gray eyes hold her gaze for a tenth of a second?

"Reverend."

Reverend Sorenson turned his attention to Betsy. "Reckon we are behind on the delivery, so Adam and I will have to take the food and eat it on the road."

"Give me just a moment, Matthias, and I will have it ready."

Annalise stared out the window. Why had Mr. Woods not entered the house with Reverend Sorenson? Why had he remained in the wagon, swiveling his head about as if on the lookout for something or someone?

A slight movement in the back of the wagon caught Annalise's eye. She fixated upon the canvas tarp covering the goods to be hauled to the next town. Annalise moved closer to the window and leaned her head toward the glass. Was an animal in the back of the wagon? Something moved again, an ever-so-slight ripple under the tarp.

"Miss Van Houten?"

Reverend Sorenson's voice interrupted her investigation. Without taking her eyes from the tarp, she answered with a simple, "Yes, Reverend?"

"What is it you are staring at?"

"I seem to detect some movement in the back of your wagon."

"Movement, you say?"

"Yes. There it is again."

Just then, a dark head came from under the tarp. Annalise saw the full features of a man. Mr. Woods abruptly turned, said something to the man, and the man again hid beneath the tarp.

"Reverend, did you know there's a man in the back of your wagon?"

Reverend Sorenson squinted out the window.

"And Mr. Woods just spoke with him."

Betsy and Reverend Sorenson shared a knowing glance and the reverend shook his head, as if answering an unspoken question.

"Here's the meal, Matthias. Have a safe trip." Betsy excused herself and rushed to the side of the wagon. Mr. Woods planted a hurried kiss on his wife's waiting lips.

"Miss Van Houten, I reckon you won't repeat anything about possibly seeing something in the back of the wagon. Do I have your word?"

Possibly seeing? My eyes certainly did not deceive me.

Was it more of a request or a demand? Annalise had never heard Reverend Sorenson take on such a somber tone. Even when he spoke of serious matters in his sermons.

"I won't say a word of it to anyone."

"You will put countless lives at risk if you mention anything you have seen, or imagined that you saw."

"I certainly didn't imagine seeing anything. I did, however, see a man poking his head up from under the tarp. A slave to be exact."

Reverend Sorenson appeared to be pondering his next words. He took a deep breath. "I pray you say nothing of what you saw here today, Miss Van Houten."

Who would she tell? It wasn't as though she had many friends in Ridge Gap, and she rarely spoke of anything of real importance to Uncle Phineas or Aunt Lavinia. "Why are you transporting a slave?"

"Sometimes the Lord calls us to save a life. It is my prayer that you don't jeopardize that."

"Reverend Sorenson, I know about the Faith Train. I overheard you, Betsy, Mr. Woods, and the other men speaking of it. But believe me, I won't breathe a word to anyone. I've also figured out that the clothes I am sewing are for the runaways. Am I correct?"

Reverend Sorenson's concern was apparent in his troubled features. "How do I know I can trust you?"

"Rest assured, you can trust me. I like slavery no more than you do."

"How can that be when your uncle owns more slaves than anyone in the area?"

The insinuation caused Annalise's face to warm. "I am aware of Uncle Phineas's wicked ways, and I assure you that I am nothing like him."

"Bets never should have allowed you to sew clothes with her today."

Annalise prayed she could tamp down the anger that rose within her. "Whyever not?"

"Because if she hadn't, you would not have seen the cargo. We should never have been so careless."

"Reverend Sorenson, please believe that I will not tell a soul about the cargo."

His voice was soft, barely above a whisper, and he leaned closer and looked Annalise directly in the eye. "I *must* be able to trust you."

Annalise wasted not a moment in her response. "You can."

Reverend Sorenson eyed her with mistrust before hurrying to the wagon. Within minutes, he and Mr. Woods traveled out of sight.

Leaving Annalise to wonder if the reverend believed a word she had promised.

Less than an hour later, barking dogs interrupted Annalise's focused attention on her sewing. She and Betsy were nearly finished for the day, and Nehemiah would be arriving any moment to retrieve her. Betsy hadn't spoken a word about the slave or about the "delivery."

And Annalise hadn't asked.

Her mind still pondered over and over Reverend Sorenson's words. He didn't trust Annalise, and oh, how she wanted to earn his trust.

"Oh dear!" exclaimed Betsy. "Try not to speak much. These men are rather abrupt and awful in their accusations."

"What men?"

Before Betsy could answer, two men on horseback with dogs yapping at their heels stopped at the house and pounded on the door.

Betsy's nervous demeanor from just seconds before switched into a relaxed and calm disposition. Holding herself with considerable poise, she stood and opened the front door. "May I help you?"

"Yes." The first man scowled. "We're bounty hunters lookin' for a runaway slave."

The other man nodded, but said nothing. Instead, he perused the room.

"The slave is about yay high," the first man said, holding his hand in the air above his own head. "Large nose, missing a front tooth. Have you seen him?"

"I have not. My friend here and I have been sewing all morning, and it's been rather quiet."

"How 'bout we come in?" Without awaiting Betsy's answer, the two men forced their way into the house, nearly toppling Betsy off her feet.

"My husband and brother will be returning soon." Betsy fetched the rifle from its place.

"No need for weapons, ma'am. We're just lookin' for a fugitive slave is all."

"I've told you I haven't seen him." Betsy kept the rifle trained on the men, and Annalise had no doubt her friend would use it.

Annalise's heart raced. The men could mean them harm and no one would hear their cries for help.

"Have you seen a runaway slave?" the man asked, edging closer to Annalise. The foul stench of his breath, combined with dank body odor, nearly made her vomit.

Lord, please make my voice calm. "I have not. But I will keep my eyes open for such a person."

"You sure neither of you ain't seen him? A farmer down the road told us he saw the slave come this way. There's a hefty reward for him."

"We have not seen him," said Annalise, grateful that her voice did not quiver.

"If you do see him, you be sure to let us know. We'll be stoppin' back by this evenin' or tomorra mornin'."

"We will do that," answered Betsy.

The men and their dogs retreated, leaving Annalise quite sure her legs might topple right out from beneath her. "What a frightening experience."

"Yes, it was."

"I take it those men have come here before?"

"Until today, never when Adam and Matthias weren't here."

"Betsy, please answer me honestly: are you, your husband, and Reverend Sorenson part of the Faith Train?"

Betsy offered a stoic expression.

"Reverend Sorenson doesn't trust me not to tell anyone. I would never do that. Never would I put lives at risk."

Betsy sighed. "I know you wouldn't Annalise. You proved that today."

Now if only Annalise could persuade Reverend Sorenson to believe her.

Chapter Four

Annalise heard him before she saw him when his abrasive voice echoed through the front parlor.

She cringed.

Dale Hiram, the son of the wealthy Luther Hiram, and one of the most calloused men Annalise had ever had the misfortune to meet, was a guest at the Thorn Plantation.

Annalise attempted to scuttle past the front parlor and up the stairs to her room.

She didn't succeed.

"Annalise, is that you?"

She stopped, one foot on the bottom stair, and held her breath. If she failed to answer, would Aunt Lavinia forego the question?

"Annalise, come into the front parlor," demanded Uncle Phineas, his obnoxious voice booming throughout the house.

Annalise squared her shoulders and gathered her courage.

And prayed.

Dale Hiram sat at the far edge of the parlor, his cognac-colored eyes seeming to stare right through her as she entered the room.

"Aunt Lavinia, Uncle Phineas, Mr. Hiram," she greeted.

Aunt Lavinia nodded toward Annalise. "Do come in and sit a spell. Mr. Hiram is here as our honored guest."

Honored guest, indeed. Annalise did her best not to show her true opinion of the man she had met thrice before. She sat on the settee and placed her hands in her lap.

"Mr. Hiram here has been discussing his interest in both the Thorn and Hiram futures. As you know, he is quite wealthy in his own right. Furthering that wealth would be of substantial benefit to both the Thorns and Hirams."

Of course. Uncle Phineas could think only of monetary topics and the furtherance of his already-massive wealth.

"I've been successful in obtaining more acreage and more slaves. Soon, I will be the wealthiest man in the entire state." Mr. Hiram steepled his fingers and leaned back against the chair.

If you think you are being impressive, Mr. Hiram, you are sorely mistaken.

Mr. Hiram leered at Annalise, his eyes traveling from her head to her toes and stopping somewhere in the middle. An eerie grin formed on his overly-thin lips.

Although the temperature in the mansion was far from frigid, Annalise shivered.

One look at Uncle Phineas, Aunt Lavinia, and Mr. Hiram brought Annalise a frightening revelation. They intended for her to be courted by the very man she despised.

Chapter Five

"Miss Van Houten?" Annalise was nearly out the church door to wait for Nehemiah when she heard Reverend Sorenson's voice.

"Hello, Reverend." Warmth crept up her face. Why did he have this odd effect on her? It wasn't as though he liked her. He certainly didn't trust her.

"Tell me, what brings you to Ridge Gap Bible Church?"

Annalise shifted and peered out the door. Was Nehemiah here to retrieve her? Best not delay if he was. Aunt Lavinia and Uncle Phineas having to wait even for a minute could cause them to decide she couldn't attend the church of her choice. "I appreciate your profound sermons, Reverend."

Reverend Sorenson eyed her with suspicion. Did he wonder why she continued to gander about, searching for the Thorn carriage? "Thank you. It's important to me to preach directly from the Bible."

"And you do a fine job of it, to be sure." Annalise took another glimpse out the church door. No sign of

Nehemiah yet. Perhaps Aunt Lavinia had been delayed while speaking with one of her friends.

"So how is it that you came to live with Mr. and Mrs. Thorn?" His voice wasn't accusatory, but there was a slight edge to his words.

"Aunt Lavinia is my father's sister. When my parents died, I came to live with them. I unfortunately had no other choice."

His handsome face still held suspicion, but that shouldn't surprise Annalise. Many in Ridge Gap weren't fond of Uncle Phineas and his pompous and vile personality.

"I'm sorry about your parents." His expression softened with compassion.

"I am nothing like the Thorns." Had those words just passed from her lips?

"I would reckon not."

Had his opinion of her changed since that day at Betsy's house? That would relieve Annalise. His opinion mattered to her. She again peered out the door.

"Are you looking for someone?"

"Yes. Unfortunately, if I am not ready to leave right when Nehemiah arrives at the door, I may not be able to attend this church in the future."

"We wouldn't want that. *I* wouldn't want that."

Reverend Sorenson's gaze held hers.

And Annalise's heart beat faster, if that were possible.

People waved their goodbyes as they passed, but Reverend Sorenson remained standing directly in front of Annalise.

Peculiar that she found herself rather enjoying their camaraderie. "This church reminds me a lot of the church I attended with my parents when I lived in Virginia."

Reverend Sorenson's mouth turned upward. "Might I take that as a compliment?"

She returned his smile. "Absolutely, Reverend, for it is a compliment, to be sure."

At that moment two things happened. One, Nehemiah arrived with the carriage. And two, the conversation marked a turning point in Annalise and Reverend Sorenson's association.

Over the next three weeks, Matthias found himself looking forward to seeing Annalise Van Houten at church. They had decided to call each other by their given names and had spoken about a variety of topics during their few precious moments while Annalise waited to be retrieved by the Thorns.

The Thorns.

While Matthias had grown fond of Annalise, her relationship with Phineas Thorn concerned him. Surely someone as likeable, smart, and lovely as Annalise wouldn't betray him and the Faith Train. Would she?

And beautiful she was. There was no doubt that Matthias was drawn to her. If only he could trust her.

CHAPTER SIX

OVER THE NEXT FEW weeks, Annalise and Betsy grew closer, and Annalise began to see more of Matthias. At times he would assist Adam on the small farm. At other times, Matthias mentioned taking deliveries or visiting those who needed his assistance. Annalise knew what that meant due to her accidental eavesdropping. If only the reverend would trust her to help with the runaways.

And be a part of the Faith Train.

Then maybe she would be making a difference in the lives of others too.

What would he say if she asked him?

Annalise wandered out to the porch when she heard Matthias's wagon approach. Perhaps if she caught the reverend after one of his "deliveries," he might be amenable to granting her request.

"Good afternoon, Annalise." Matthias flashed her a handsome smile and she did her best to maintain her composure. Goodness, if the man wasn't dapper! There was something about him that caused a pleasant, jittery sensation deep within her stomach.

With a struggle, Annalise reminded herself of the task she wished to undertake. "Good afternoon, Matthias."

"Reckon I've been on my feet most of the day. Care to sit a spell?" Matthias gestured to the two chairs on the porch. "I want to thank you for not telling the bounty hunters about the cargo in the wagon." He paused. "Betsy told me."

The admiration in his voice touched her. "You are welcome. Was the man a runaway?"

He said nothing, but his expression clouded with turmoil. Matthias sighed. "Annalise, your parents owned slaves, correct?"

Matthias must have discussed this with Betsy, for other than Annalise's aunt and uncle, only Betsy knew. "Yes, but—"

"Then it's possible that you might have the same opinion about owning slaves."

"My parents were quite different than Uncle Phineas." Annalise struggled to keep her voice low. How dare Matthias insinuate that her parents were evil like her uncle!

"Truth is truth, Annalise. You live at the plantation and see the treatment the slaves receive. Phineas Thorn is known for being one of the most brutal slave masters in the state, and you are his niece."

Annalise felt the color rising in her cheeks. "I do not know how to convince you that I am *nothing* like Uncle Phineas. My parents owned slaves, yes. But they treated them kindly and with dignity. I grew up with the friendship of two of them—Jinny and Tandey. Who, by the way,

I would love to see escape. To suggest that I am like my uncle is the worst misrepresentation of the truth I have ever known—a complete falsehood!" She stood. "I best be gathering my sewing items. Nehemiah will be here soon."

Matthias stood and reached for her arm. "Annalise, please understand. I must be cautious. So many lives are at stake."

"If only you knew how I detest the prospect of slavery. While I am not a slave, I do know a thing or two about lack of freedom, for I experience it every day. Mind you, it is nothing like the slavery you seek to eradicate, but it is a form of bondage I shall endeavor to escape from. They even intend to tell me whom I shall marry." The thought of Dale Hiram disturbed her.

Her pulse raced and her mouth grew dry. Matthias's insinuation brought about a range of emotions from anger and sadness to frustration and anguish.

"Annalise." He fixed his gaze on hers. "I'm sorry if I offended you. You must understand."

"While I am not usually prone to temper, I'll not understand your position in accusing me of being someone I am not."

Matthias took a deep breath. "All right then. Yes. The man you saw was a runaway."

His remark caught her unawares. Did he finally believe her? Feeling guilty that it took nothing short of a tirade to convince him, Annalise offered a prayer seeking forgiveness— combined with a prayer of gratitude. "And is the runaway—the cargo—is he safe now?"

"That I don't know. My role is only to transport them to the next place and pray. God takes care of it from there."

"So you do not know the other people aiding the runaways?"

"Not beyond our group in Ridge Gap. It's safer that way."

"Might you have a position for me within the organization?"

A flicker of something crossed his face. Uncertainty perhaps? Lingering fragments of mistrust and doubt? "Annalise, you need to understand that being a part of the Faith Train can be dangerous. If someone is caught aiding a slave's escape, they can be jailed, flogged, hanged, or worse."

"I'm willing to take that chance. I desire to serve the Lord in this way and make a difference."

"There aren't any open positions."

"Surely, Matthias, there must be something I can do."

Matthias rubbed his chin. "You can assist by continuing to sew clothes for the runaways. But you cannot tell anyone, Annalise. I'm taking a risk just by telling—and involving—you."

"I won't tell a soul." She paused, grateful for the change in his opinion of her. She truly wanted him to think well of her. "But are you sure there isn't something more I can do? It seems so insignificant."

His kind eyes searched hers. "It is far from insignificant. Each part done to aid this cause is important. Each person on the Faith Train has a different role to perform.

If one role remained unfulfilled, the entire plan would fail." He paused. "Are you familiar with First Corinthians 12:12-27? It discusses how each part of the body is important and no less critical than any other part—just as each person in the body of Christ. So it is with the Faith Train. Sewing clothes for the runaways is as important as transporting them. It's just a different role."

"I only want to make a difference in the lives of others."

"You are, Annalise. You are."

Matthias's words meant more to her than she could ever explain.

CHAPTER SEVEN

Over the following weeks, Annalise spent more time at Betsy's house sewing clothes for the runaways. Aunt Lavinia continued to believe it was a sewing circle, and Annalise prayed the Lord would forgive her for omitting the complete truth.

And lying about the man in the wagon.

Matthias had given a sermon last Sunday about how, while God does not excuse lying, it can be necessary to save a life. As did Miriam and Rahab in the Old Testament.

Not only was Annalise aiding the Faith Train, but she was also coming to know a great deal more about the man who was winning her heart.

A man of the cloth named Matthias Sorenson.

"Care for a walk?" Matthias asked one afternoon.

Annalise set down her sewing needle and fabric. Today had been productive. "I would love a walk."

Together they strolled through the privacy of Betsy and Adam's property. The birds chirped and the air smelled of pine. "Thank you for your hard work on the clothing."

"I'm thrilled to be putting my skills to good use. My mother would be proud."

"You miss your parents."

"I do. They were dear people who loved the Lord and were taken home far too soon. What about you? Where are your parents?"

"They are in Ohio."

"And do they work for the Faith Train as well?"

Matthias shot her one of his grins. "Yes, they do. But again—"

"It's a secret. I know. Have I ever, in the two months I've been assisting, shared any information with anyone?"

"Reckon you haven't." He offered his elbow and she placed her hand through it. It felt natural to be walking through the forest with him. She had grown to appreciate his wisdom, his sense of humor, and his passion for assisting the downtrodden.

They stopped a short distance in front of the river. "They say that when the runaways cross the Ohio River, they are crossing the Jordan River," he said, watching the clear water trickle over the rocks.

"I can see the reason they say that."

"As can I." He turned toward her and took both of her hands in his.

Annalise figured her heart might stop right then and there.

"Annalise, I know we come from different stations in life, but I enjoy spending time with you."

"I do too, Matthias."

"If we are ever caught in what we do…"

"God will protect us."

"Annalise, if we are ever caught in what we do…if it is God's will that we are caught, promise me something." He brushed his thumb over the top of her hand.

Her knees felt weak from his touch. How could she even speak at a moment like this? "All right," she whispered.

"Promise me you will not come forward and state your role on the Faith Train. Act as though you know nothing. Promise me."

"But what if you go to jail…or worse?"

"Promise me you won't tell of your involvement. I need your word, Annalise."

"I—"

"Promise me."

"All right, Matthias, I promise you, but…" *I've grown quite fond of you and wouldn't want to see anything happen to you.*

"Thank you."

They stood facing each other. Annalise wished he would kiss her. Wished they could court each other and plan a future.

For he was the man she was quickly growing to love.

Matthias wished he could kiss her. Not a tiny peck, but a true kiss telling of his affection for her. During the many hours spent with her at Betsy and Adam's house and those times spent after church services while she awaited her ride home, Matthias had grown fond of her company. She amused him with her sense of humor. Tugged at his heart with her tenderness toward the slaves. And her beauty was an added benefit.

If only they could court. But it wasn't possible. He was a poor preacher who didn't even own a home. And she was a wealthy heiress whose aunt and uncle expected her to marry well.

Still, he would dream...and pray about such an opportunity with the woman of his affection.

Without a second thought, Matthias reached over and stroked her cheek. Her blue eyes gazing back at him were almost his undoing. What would it be like to spend every moment with her? To love her and care for her? To have her as his partner, not only in marriage, but also in his work on the Faith Train?

Don't be a cad, Matthias. Such thoughts are too unlikely for you to even consider.

"Matthias, what will I do if they make me marry Dale Hiram?"

"Dale Hiram?" Matthias shook from his daydream of loving Annalise forever to the unpleasant thought of one of his biggest enemies.

"I fear Aunt Lavinia will insist we court. I cannot court him, Matthias. I *cannot.*"

"Surely they would not force you to marry someone you do not love."

"You don't know them." Tear glistened in her eyes.

That couldn't happen. Not when he wanted to court her and someday make her his wife.

Whoa. Marriage? Matthias shook his head. Too soon for such thoughts. But didn't a man sometimes know—truly know—that God had picked someone just for him, even after a short while?

Annalise shifted and at that moment, and without another thought, he took her into his arms. He knew not what to say to alleviate her fears of having to marry Dale Hiram. He knew not how to solve what could become a horrible life sentence for Annalise.

So instead, he held her close, never wanting to let her go.

Chapter Eight

ANNALISE HEARD VOICES DOWNSTAIRS and cringed. She always detested it when Luther Hiram, Dale Hiram, Edgar Oret, and her uncle had their "secret" meetings. Coarse words and copious imbibing always took place. Slaves, especially the women, were even more mistreated by Uncle Phineas and his cronies during these "secret" meetings. She dared not be in their presence during these times. Even Aunt Lavinia found somewhere else to be. Annalise cocked her ear toward the conversations and thought she heard an additional voice.

She tried to identify the voice. She hadn't heard it often, but it seemed familiar.

Then it came to her.

Sheriff Bleyer.

The thought of the lawman participating in the evil Uncle Phineas and his friends concocted made Annalise's heart race and her thoughts multiply. She had always suspected there was something not quite right about Sheriff Bleyer, even more so after his interrogation about her church attendance.

Annalise crept down the staircase as quietly as she could manage. Her stockinged feet padded on the wood steps as she gripped the handrail.

As if it could protect her.

She remained on the alert, glancing frequently to and fro as she proceeded toward the library where the men were.

"I know there's somethin' goin' on with that Reverend Matthias," said Sheriff Bleyer. Then a pause. "Pour me another drink, Phineas."

"Good thing your deputy is handling matters tonight, Bleyer. Wouldn't do you any good to get caught drunk," chortled Luther Hiram.

Annalise heard the chink of a bottle hitting a glass. She kept her head pressed against the wall, even though the temptation to jut her neck forward a bit and see what was going on was almost impossible to resist.

"I agree with you on the good reverend," snarled Uncle Phineas. "He's too friendly toward slaves. Even saw him helping one who had dropped her load of parcels from the mercantile once. I say we do something about it."

Sheriff Bleyer sounded too eager when he answered, "Like what?"

"You're the corrupt sheriff, you think of something," snapped Luther. "If we get him out of the way, the church will no longer be a problem. I reckon there are others in that *place of worship* that should be hung for assisting slaves."

"Don't your niece go there?" Edgar Oret asked.

"Yah, I seen her there 'afore," said Sheriff Bleyer. "Asked her about it once. She didn't give no indication she thought somethin' was amiss. But then, she don't seem like the most intelligent woman."

Annalise narrowed her eyes. She was indeed an intelligent woman! For just that comment, she ought to let Sheriff Bleyer know her opinion. But she stuffed down the pride that reared within her and continued to listen to the conversation.

Dale Hiram slurred his words. Too much whisky perhaps? From the odor floating up the stairs, it would appear the men had overindulged in cigars as well. "Why don't y'all do something about that niece of yours, Phineas? Make her stop going to church or something?"

Annalise bristled. No one, not even the tyrannical and dictatorial Uncle Phineas, would stop her from attending church and worshipping God.

"Don't you see, Dale? Having her there can help us."

"How so?"

"She can be a spy of sorts."

Never.

Sheriff Bleyer let loose a mean laugh. "No way is she gonna agree to that. She ain't like you, Phineas."

"True. She is too much like Lavinia's brother." Uncle Phineas's voice rang harsh in Annalise's ears. "A pathetic coward, if there ever was one."

How dare you!

In apparent preparation of spitting, Luther Hiram expectorated, an offensive sound that made Annalise cringe. Pity the slave who would have to spend an inordinate amount of time scrubbing the hardened sputum from the wood floor. "Can't believe you don't make that girl mind you better. If you'd force her to marry Dale, all this would be solved. She would finally be controlled the way she ought to be."

The thought of marrying Dale Hiram sent shivers of disgust from Annalise's head to her toes.

A sound made Annalise jump, causing her to smack her head against the wall.

"What was that noise?" Luther asked.

"I'll go take a look-see," offered Sheriff Bleyer.

Annalise sucked in her breath. If she thought marrying Dale Hiram a nightmare, she could only imagine what Uncle Phineas and his cronies would do to her if they discovered her eavesdropping on the stairs.

With the swiftness of a doe, Annalise retreated upstairs to her room. She was certain everyone on the plantation heard her pounding heart, especially her uncle.

Loud footsteps barged up the stairs. Would they find her? Realize she was the one they heard? Punish her?

Lord, please, I beg of You to protect me.

"Don't see no one," announced Sheriff Bleyer.

Annalise let out the breath she had been holding and prayed for serenity.

Moments later, she opened the door and poked her head into the hallway. No sign of Aunt Lavinia. Good. The woman was still reclining in her room.

The sounds of the men had grown louder. Annalise took a step into the hallway, keeping her hand on the doorknob of her room. For what? Security perhaps?

"Since we believe the good reverend is to blame for these most recent escapes, there is only one solution." Annalise shuddered at the cruelty in Uncle Phineas's voice.

Luther cleared his throat. "What's that?"

"We hang him for his crimes."

The men joined in a chorus of vile laughter.

"Let's enjoy the rest of our evening, shall we? Tomorrow night, we'll discuss plans to rid ourselves of that gutless namby-pamby once and for all."

"Here! Here!"

Annalise froze. She must, no matter what the cost, listen to the men's conversation tomorrow. Then she would share with Matthias what she had learned.

Lord, grant me courage.

Not to intervene would surely put Matthias's life at risk.

Annalise tiptoed to her door and cracked it open. She had wanted a somewhat-peaceful evening reading a book in the library or knitting in the parlor. She missed those quiet times of togetherness with her parents.

They would never again be possible.

And there would be no peace while she resided at the Thorn residence.

The knocker on the front door had sounded at half past seven. Sheriff Bleyer, followed by the Hirams and Edgar Oret, entered the mansion.

Annalise had spent much time praying in preparation for this very moment.

The moment when she uncovered her uncle's plan to have Matthias put to death because of his work with the Faith Train.

Surely, Lord, that is not Your will. Matthias has been such an instrument in assisting the slaves to freedom. Lord, I beseech you to preserve his life.

The men gathered in the library, and Annalise envisioned Uncle Phineas taking the most comfortable spot in the room, the leather chair adjacent to his cherry wood desk. Rather than use the desk for writing, as most folks did, Uncle Phineas would prop his large feet on top of it, scuffing the fine wood.

It wouldn't have mattered so much if the desk hadn't been Father's cherished writing desk. The desk where he so eloquently penned poems for Mother.

A loud clomping noise sounded—Uncle Phineas's feet on the desk, perhaps? She imagined him settling his rotund self into the leather chair and tipping the whisky flask toward his mouth.

"Gentlemen, thank you for joining me on this fine evening."

Uncle Phineas's voice made Annalise's blood curdle. *This fine evening? The evening when you unveil your vile plans to take someone's life?*

"I've been doin' some followin' of our good reverend," said Sheriff Bleyer. "Seems he does have a way with the colored folk. Like they trust him or somethin'."

"What do you mean?"

"Yesterday, he walked by a slave and tugged on his right ear. Had to be some sorta code or somethin'. Reckon the slave seemed to understand what the good reverend was doin' for he nodded and went on his way."

"Doesn't surprise me none," interjected Luther. "Whenever folks engage in illegal activities, a shroud of deceit under the cloak of a code seems reasonable."

Uncle Phineas interrupted Luther with a curse toward one of the slaves, demanding she retrieve him something to eat.

Likely Jinny. Poor, poor dear.

Unfortunately, that wasn't the worst the young slave woman had experienced at the hands of Uncle Phineas.

"Where were we? Oh, yes, discussing a secret code between the good reverend and a slave. That's right fine investigative work, Sheriff. Didn't think you had it in you."

Rather than take offense, Sheriff Bleyer chuckled. "Even a man with no law trainin' can do some investigatin' when the moment calls for it."

"Our goal is to prove that Reverend Sorenson is guilty. He has some friends that might look unkindly upon us apprehending the man and tossing him into jail for a hanging the following day," said Dale.

Annalise strained to hear the voices. Dale's, especially, was lower and more foreboding. Schooled at the best of universities, and now a rich plantation owner, according to Aunt Lavinia, he would be the perfect match for Annalise.

Especially to secure the family fortune.

Annalise winced. For one, there was likely nothing left of her family's fortune. Secondly, the only man worse than Dale Hiram was Uncle Phineas. Even Luther wasn't as bad as his evil son.

And Luther Hiram was a reprobate if there ever was one.

Sneaking forward as quietly as she could, Annalise was taken aback by the new portrait of her uncle hanging in the hallway.

Startling at the glooming glare of Phineas Thorn, Annalise jumped back. The floor creaked.

"Miss, are you all right?"

Annalise jumped again at Jinny's voice, as she rushed down the hallway with a stack of clean linens. Annalise held a finger to her mouth and shook her head.

The slave woman appeared to understand. She nodded and went on her way.

But not before Annalise saw the bruise darkening beneath Jinny's left eye.

Jinny had to be next to know the taste of freedom.

Annalise slid against the wall again and did her best to listen to the conversation on the floor beneath her. The men had, unfortunately, lowered their voices.

Or perhaps Uncle Phineas had closed the door to the library.

Whatever the reason, Annalise struggled to make out any of the words being exchanged between the men.

Chapter Nine

Annalise took another step down the staircase. Then another.

Lord, please keep me safe.

She held her breath all the while her heart raced. Where was Aunt Lavinia? Would she emerge at any moment and catch Annalise attempting to eavesdrop?

"Now that's an idea and a half," Uncle Phineas thundered.

What idea?

She must move closer.

"Annalise!"

Annalise straightened her posture and scurried up the stairs to her room.

"Annalise!"

"Yes, Aunt Lavinia?"

"Oh, there you are." Aunt Lavinia patted her curly gray hair.

Annalise willed her heart to be still. What if Aunt Lavinia had found her on the stairs? What if...

"You look bedraggled, Annalise."

The statement was more of a chastisement than a concern. Just like most of Aunt Lavinia's comments.

"I was just preparing to retire for the night."

Lord, forgive me for me for that bold untruth.

"I see. Well, I thought I heard some clamor. Is everything quite all right?"

"Quite all right, Aunt Lavinia."

"Very well. It must have been your uncle and his unruly friends."

"Indeed."

Aunt Lavinia eyed Annalise with suspicion. "Good night, then."

"Good night, Aunt Lavinia."

Please hurry and retire to your room so I can return to hear the men's plans.

Taking one more glance back at Annalise, Aunt Lavinia proceeded to her bedchamber. A few moments later, Annalise heard the door close and lock.

Perhaps, Annalise hoped, the men would be drunk and would repeat their plans. She waited a few more minutes, anxiety permeating every ounce of her being. *Lord, grant me the wisdom to know when it is safe to eavesdrop again.*

With the utmost prudence, Annalise skulked down the long hall and to the top of the stairs, all the while keeping a close watch on Aunt Lavinia's door. The men's rowdy voices carried up the stairs, although Annalise was unable to discern their words. For the third time in as many days, she continued carefully down the stairs and toward the library until she could distinguish their words.

"It's a task that must be undertaken."

How much had she missed due to Aunt Lavinia's "concern?"

"I agree. Who we gonna use as the bait?"

Bait?

"How about my slave, Horace? The reverend doesn't know him, from what I recollect."

"This might just work. Yes, Dale, let's use Horace. Give him the details tomorrow. He'll be more than happy to do it," Uncle Phineas added.

"I'll tell Horace to act as if he wants his freedom. He'll seek the good reverend out and ask if he can assist him in his endeavor to escape. Horace will do his best to convince Reverend Sorenson that he needs his freedom. Isn't that how it all works?" Dale snarled. "Horace is a good-for-nothing slave as it is."

"And," added Luther, "Reverend Sorenson is a good-for-nothing preacher, so it's the perfect match for a perfect plan."

Annalise gasped, covering her mouth with her hand. *This plan mustn't succeed.*

"Good. Then he's perfect for the job. Sheriff Bleyer, be at the ready to bring Reverend Sorenson to the Ridge Gap town square after he decides to help our decoy. Luther and Edgar, you start the crowds rioting about the injustice of one of our own—a reverend of all things—breaking the law. It won't take much to bring the reverend to justice. Folks won't stand for a criminal on the streets of Ridge Gap, preacher or not. As Lavinia would say, 'it's absolutely scandalous.'"

The men chuckled at Uncle Phineas's comment.

Anger rose within Annalise. How dare they make unkind comments about Matthias. And how dare they plot the murder of an innocent man. She had every mind to barge into the library and rebuke them in the harshest way possible.

Much as the ideal held appeal, it would be futile. They would likely throw her in jail for being a sympathizer. Then where would Matthias be? How could she assist the man she was growing to love?

And how could she aid in the escape of more slaves?

Instead of giving into the temptation, Annalise retreated to her room.

She had an eventful day tomorrow.

CHAPTER TEN

GOD'S MERCY WAS UPON her with Uncle Phineas and Aunt Lavinia in town for the day.

Lord, please alleviate the case of nerves permeating through me.

For if she failed at her attempt to warn Matthias, his life—and the lives of others, including her own—would be at stake.

Annalise swung open the barn door. Tandey, the stable slave was grooming Annalise's black horse, Eclipse. "Good afternoon, Tandey," Annalise greeted him with a low voice. "I would care to take Eclipse on a ride."

"Will it be the sidesaddle for you, Miss?" A glimmer shone in the young slave's eye as he reached for the saddle and placed it on Eclipse's back.

"Yes, Tandey," Annalise answered with her own smirk. Besides Annalise and her father, Tandey was the only other person who knew that Annalise had, on more than one occasion, ridden bareback. The memory of Father allowing Annalise to ride bareback with him through the vast fields of the Van Houten property while Mother attended a tea party warmed Annalise's heart. He had allowed it thrice more, on the condition that no one must know that he, Hayes Van Houten III, had allowed his well-bred, high-society daughter and only child, to partake in such an unladylike activity.

Annalise, of course, had agreed. Tandey, barely four years older than her and a slave who had been born on the Van Houten Plantation, had taken particular delight in Father's demand for secrecy. He had laughed for minutes, as he watched Annalise clutched the thoroughbred's mane.

Mother would have had suffered from the vapors had she known the truth about Annalise and the bareback rides on those hot summer days so long ago. It was the only secret Annalise held from her beloved mother. A necessary secret as Mother, bless her heart, wasn't nearly as forward in her thinking as Annalise was.

Four times riding bareback for several hours—each time without the irritation of that bothersome sidesaddle—had made Annalise practically an expert. Under Father's patient guidance, Annalise had been convinced she could win a riding contest against the best of the best.

Although Father hadn't been *that* permissive.

Annalise smiled at the memory, thankful for the reprieve from the burdens that overwhelmed her.

Moments later, she rode slowly through the barn door and out into the open. Glancing down to ensure that her riding habit was draped carefully over her ankles, Annalise continued past slaves picking cotton in the fields, past the creek, and past the pecan grove. Riding sidesaddle was a torturously slow process.

Annalise did her best to act as though nothing was amiss on this hot and rather humid day. She held her head high, as she'd been taught in those riding classes Mother enrolled her in from a young age.

The sun was high in the sky, indicating that Annalise didn't have much time before her aunt and uncle returned home. She must hurry if she desired to be effective in her discreet warning to Matthias.

How can one hurry with this most ridiculous excuse for a saddle?

Eclipse neighed as if he heard her question and agreed.

Some miles later, Annalise spied the cluster of trees she sought. Pulling gently on the reins, she brought Eclipse to a stop and dismounted. Then, methodically, albeit swiftly, Annalise removed the saddle and hid it safely in the center of the trees, covering it with grasses and branches to disguise its presence.

She again mounted Eclipse, thankful for the pair of tan trousers beneath her riding habit. With a light tap of her heel to his flank, Eclipse took off at a gallop. Annalise clutched the reins, welcoming the warm breeze.

Lord, please don't allow anyone to see me.

Rarely had anyone taken the short-cut through the forest, a path Annalise was thankful to have stumbled on while out for a walk one day.

She ducked her head as low tree branches hovered. Birds chirped and the smell of wildflowers filled the air.

If only she could be free like this all the time, without the constraints of Aunt Lavinia and Uncle Phineas and their desire to marry her off to someone like the abhorrent Dale Hiram.

Think not of Mr. Hiram right now. There are more demanding tasks at hand.

So instead, Annalise thought of Matthias as she rode briskly through the trees. She thought of his warm gray eyes and his handsome smile. Of his servant's heart and his desire for justice. Of his strong arms and dapper appearance.

Of how he had almost kissed her.

Or so she had thought. Maybe Annalise had imagined it.

Either way, no matter who her aunt and uncle desired for her to court and marry, Annalise's heart would forever belong to Matthias Sorenson.

Which was why she must reach him and warn him of the slave bait her uncle and his comrades had concocted.

It wouldn't be much further now to Betsy and Adam's house. Annalise urged Eclipse to gallop faster, and Annalise leaned low, pretending that she was one of the contestants in the bareback races Father had taken her to during the town's Founder's Day.

Only this race was for a life.

Chapter Eleven

MATTHIAS HEARD HER BEFORE he saw her. A vision of beauty astride a black horse tearing through the pasture toward his sister's house. He rubbed his eyes and did a double-take.

"Annalise?"

A mixture of elation and concern filled Matthias. Why was the woman he had recently grown so fond of riding toward Betsy's home? And bareback?

"There's something wrong," he muttered.

Betsy joined him on the porch. "Now, now, Matthias. Don't always think the worst."

"No, Bets, there is something wrong." Matthias felt it in his entire being. He marched down the two steps of the porch and hurried to meet Annalise. From the look on her face as she drew nearer, Matthias knew his assumption was correct.

Something threatened the Faith Train and his role in it.

"Matthias!" Her voice alone caused him concern.

"Annalise? Is everything all right?"

"May we step inside?"

Even though she had apparently ridden a great distance from her home to his, her beauty had not been compromised. A strand of blond hair cascaded near her right cheek, and Matthias resisted the urge to reach for it.

It was her uneven breath that came in almost-gasps that caught his attention. "Are you all right?"

"Please sit and have some tea," Betsy offered.

"I regret that I don't have the time for formalities, but thank you just the same, Betsy."

Her face showed grave concern, and he longed to embrace her and tell her all would be well—to hold her in his arms and shield her from whatever burdened her.

But he couldn't very well reassure her that all would be fine.

For what if it wasn't?

Her eyes lit with fear. "Matthias, you must be careful."

"Whatever do you mean, Annalise?" Betsy moved toward her.

"Matthias's life is in danger."

"Danger?" Had he heard her correctly?

Annalise's words tumbled out in rapid succession, one word overlapping the other as she laid out the trap her uncle and his cohorts were setting to catch Matthias. She told of the slave bait plan and the prearranged riots. Annalise leaned toward him and whispered. "They know you are part of the Faith Train."

"How can they know?"

"I'm not sure." She looked at him with a troubled expression. "Wait. Surely you don't think I'm the one who revealed your role in freeing the slaves?"

Matthias shook his head. "No, Annalise, I do not think you would ever share such information intentionally. However, you may have—"

The hurt in her eyes was almost more than he could bear, and he regretted his insinuation. "Annalise, it's just that you may have unknowingly—"

"Never, Matthias, never!" Her voice went up an octave and tears streamed down her face. "You must understand that I would never lead them to you. Why would I?"

"Annalise, I'm sorry, I just...if they're watching you, as I believe Sheriff Bleyer to be doing, he may have ascertained my involvement—and yours."

"With so much at stake, I would be an utter fool to allow that."

Matthias again longed to draw her into his arms to comfort her. Only this time the comfort was for the hurt he had just caused her. "I only meant that such a mishap is possible given your uncle's suspicions of you and Sheriff Bleyer's observations of your comings and goings."

"I believe this conversation is over. Matthias, I rode out here, risking my own life, to tell you that yours is in grave danger. Don't think for a second that they will not draw you into this trap if you are not wise and disregard the slave's request. Do not give in when a slave asks for help. No matter what. Do not offer to assist him. For if you do, Uncle Phineas plans to have you hanged."

"Thank you, Annalise. Thank you for telling me. But it will be difficult for me to turn away a slave in need."

"You must. There is no other choice. It could be the very slave Uncle Phineas uses to trap you. I must go." Her voice took on a sarcastic tone Matthias had never heard from her, and her eyes narrowed. "I'm sorry if you believe I am to blame for their knowledge of your role in the Faith Train."

Before he or Betsy could respond, Annalise marched toward the door. "Goodbye, Matthias. Betsy."

Matthias wanted to go after her. He wanted to explain his error and seek her forgiveness. But she rode through the woods away from the house before he could convince his own two lethargic feet to move from where he stood.

What have I done? Lord, please forgive me.

CHAPTER TWELVE

TEARS FLOWED, SPILLING OVER her cheeks and down her neck. How could Matthias believe she had led Uncle Phineas and the others to him? Hadn't she proven herself? What more must she do to convince him?

And to think she had entertained the fanciful thought of courtship with Matthias. What a fool she had been.

Annalise continued through the woods toward home, ensuring that no one had seen nor followed her. Thankfully, she saw no one, save the creatures that made the woods their home. And Annalise heard no one except the birds chirping on the humid July day.

When she reached the place where she had hidden the saddle, Annalise stopped Eclipse and dismounted. Digging through the brush to uncover the sidesaddle, she saddled her horse, then started toward home. Glancing at the sun's position, Annalise knew she had little time before Uncle Phineas or Aunt Lavinia began to wonder to where she had ventured.

Freedom did not exist in the Thorn household. Not for the slaves and certainly not for Annalise.

She forced herself to now ride at a much slower pace than she had astride. To not do so would surely end in disaster when she was inadvertently thrown from the horse. As she rode at a sluggish speed, Annalise's mind reverted to Matthias and his accusation. Would her dried tears be evident to Aunt Lavinia? All the more reason to hurry home and into her room to wash her face before being called to the noonday meal.

Her heart broke into a thousand pieces. How could Matthias think she would ever lead Uncle Phineas or any of his cohorts to him? How could Matthias believe that Annalise would be so daft as to not ensure that no one knew of the covert operation of which she was now a part?

"Annalise, it's just that you may have unknowingly..." His words kept ringing in her ears.

"I only meant that such a mishap is possible given your uncle's suspicions of you and Sheriff Bleyer's constant observations of your comings and goings."

Annalise's heart beat even faster at the thought. Had she done something to make the sheriff suspicious? She recounted her actions from the past days and weeks.

No. She could not think of a thing that would have made Sheriff Bleyer wary of her actions.

And then the audacity... Annalise almost said those words aloud as she recounted Matthias's other words during their conversation: *"Thank you for telling me. But it will be difficult for me to turn away a slave in need."* So Annalise had risked her life in eavesdropping, further risked her life in riding a considerable distance—scandalously astride, no less—and risked her life going to tell Matthias what she had overheard.

All for naught.

Annalise gritted her teeth. Had it all been in vain? It would be if Matthias decided to help the slave posing as a potential runaway in need. Why could Matthias not heed her advice? Why was the man so obstinate?

Because he has a compassionate heart.

The reminder impressed upon her heart, but Annalise chose to ignore it. Compassionate heart or not, Matthias was downright foolish to not take seriously her words of warning.

And then to suspect her of leading Uncle Phineas and Sheriff Bleyer to the organization.

A combination of anger, irritation, and self-pity rose within Annalise. She never should have become involved in the Faith Train.

Had she even been of help?

Annalise added self-doubt to her list of emotions.

She should have never allowed her heart to be stolen by the handsome man with broad shoulders and gray eyes who preached the Word of God Sunday after Sunday.

Chapter Thirteen

THE STABLE CAME INTO view after what seemed like a lengthy trip. Annalise allowed a sigh to escape her lips. At least she was no longer crying, for the moment anyhow.

The acres and acres of plantation worked by dozens of slaves reminded her of how important her job was—even if Matthias's comment had diminished that importance in her mind.

"Annalise!"

At the sharp mention of her name, Annalise nearly fell off Eclipse. She turned to see Uncle Phineas on horseback. Had he followed her? Did he know where she had gone?

Fear rippled through her.

Uncle Phineas would not show mercy, even to a relative, if she were caught helping slaves.

Annalise willed her voice not to tremble. "Hello, Uncle Phineas."

"Where have you been?" His harsh tone stirred panic in every part of Annalise's being.

So much for pleasantries.

"I said, 'Where have you been?'"

Think quickly, Annalise...

"I have been out for a ride. Such a lovely day."

Uncle Phineas stopped his horse in front of Eclipse. "Out riding where?" His evil dark eyes bored through her.

"Out yonder."

"Yonder?"

"Yes, Uncle Phineas. Is everything quite all right?"

"That depends on you, Annalise." He practically spat her name.

No surprise there. Annalise knew Uncle Phineas's feelings for her did not include benevolence. She pondered her response. Should she feign innocence? Reply with a syrupy retort? However Annalise responded, she feared she would stir up more wrath in her volatile uncle. *Lord, please give me the words to speak.*

"It appears there is something going on that you're not telling me."

"Uncle Phineas, I merely went for a ride through your lovely property."

"Be assured, Annalise, that I will discover whatever it is you are scheming. You are not beyond the law, no matter who you are. If you are, as Sheriff Bleyer suspects, doing something to assist slaves, not only will you be punished to the fullest extent possible, but I will see to it that every slave on the plantation takes a beating for your poor choices."

Annalise bit back her trepidation. Uncle Phineas had already punished Jinny, Tandey, and the others for her wrongdoings.

"For example, I gave Tandey a good beating today for allowing you to ride by your lonesome."

"No—"

"What is it about the slaves that concerns you so, Annalise? If you think for a moment they deserve freedom, you are sorely mistaken." He waved his hand at her. A hand that Annalise feared was about to connect with her cheek. A hand that had waved many a whip toward the backs of slaves.

She jolted back, nearly falling out of the saddle.

"Get to the house, Annalise. And no more riding without a chaperone."

Panic infused her at Uncle Phineas's condemnation. "Yes, sir."

Uncle Phineas had certainly whipped Tandey. The young man groaned, as he mucked the stables. Annalise's heart broke at the sight of the lacerations and dried blood that crusted on his arms. She could only imagine what his back must look like.

Annalise breathed in with relief to see that Uncle Phineas had not followed her. She must be careful. Speaking to Tandey would only cause another whipping.

"Oh, Tandey," she whispered. "I'm so sorry."

Tandey smiled at her, his eyes kind, and nodded. "Don't worry about me none, Miss Annalise." His voice was low as well. For he knew—knew all too well—what would happen if Uncle Phineas heard him speak to Annalise.

"Someday, Tandey, I promise, I will see to it that you are freed."

Tandey assisted her from the horse. "Don't speak of that, Annalise. It could put you in danger."

"I know that, Tandey, but I promise both you and Jinny will someday be free to marry and start your own family in freedom."

A smile lit his ebony face. "If only it could be so."

"It will be, one day."

A sudden flicker in Tandey's eyes told Annalise that he dared to believe her words. Honestly, she shouldn't be making such promises. But she meant what she said. Someday her dear friends would be free.

And hopefully so would she.

Chapter Fourteen

If Annalise had hoped to slip unnoticed into her room, she was mistaken. Aunt Lavinia lurked just inside the parlor. "Is that you, Annalise?"

"Yes, ma'am."

"Goodness, but your face looks atrocious. All red and burned from the sun. Do you not know you will cause freckling from being so irresponsible?"

Annalise reached a hand up to her face. Could Aunt Lavinia see the dried tears that scarred her cheeks? "Yes, ma'am."

"Where were you anyhow? Your Uncle Phineas has the mind to punish you for taking off like that without telling a soul."

"I went on a ride about the plantation." *Sorry, Lord. I know I went beyond the plantation. Please forgive me for that minor falsehood.*

"A ride about the plantation, indeed. Does it take so long for you to do so? You do realize that your insensitive actions caused a slave to be beaten. Was it worth it, Annalise?"

Aunt Lavinia knew full well Annalise's compassion for all people, slave or free, and she chose often to use it against her niece. "It was a mere ride about the plantation. It reminded me of the times I did so with my father. *Your brother*, who was a kind and godly man."

The words came out harsher than Annalise intended, and Aunt Lavinia recoiled ever so slightly before regaining her composure.

Blame it on the dreadful day. What with the urgency of meeting with Matthias without being caught, his suspicions of her, Tandey's beating and knowing it was all her fault, and the entire ordeal of assisting runaway slaves. It was enough to thrust Annalise into a deep melancholy.

"You will not speak to me in that manner, Annalise. Remember that your uncle and I gave you a home when you were orphaned. Who else would be so patient and gracious? Your antics deserve nothing less than vagrancy. Where would you be then? Your words and your actions are drawing you ever closer to being ousted from this home. And if you are indeed contemplating assisting runaway slaves, as Phineas believes you are, you will be punished for your shenanigans. Believe you me, neither your uncle nor I will be there to rescue you from the clutches of Sheriff Bleyer."

Annalise knew that even her sun-reddened face blanched at Aunt Lavinia's words. It was one thing to be punished for her disrespect of her aunt, but quite another to be accused of assisting runaway slaves. At least Aunt Lavinia had said the word *contemplating*. Perhaps that meant that Uncle Phineas was not sure of Annalise's role in the Faith Train, but only assumed it.

Aunt Lavinia looked Annalise square in the eye. If she was awaiting an apology, it would not be forthcoming. For it wouldn't be honest, nor made with a pure heart. She bit her lip. *Lord, help me control my anger.*

"Yes, ma'am," she finally said, proud of herself that she had avoided gritting her teeth while doing so. "May I go to my room to freshen up?"

Aunt Lavinia narrowed her eyes. "Yes, you may."

Annalise plodded up the stairs, careful not to make any additional noise. Not only were her steps heavy, but her heart also. When she entered her room, she collapsed on the bed.

She grasped her feather pillow and mourned. Mourned the loss of her beloved parents. Grieved that she must reside with her aunt and uncle. Lamented over Matthias's suspicions and lack of trust. Sorrowed over the punishment Tandey had received because of her choice to go for a ride. Bemoaned her own lack of freedom.

Pushing her face into the pillow, Annalise willed the tears to stop. But they wouldn't. Sobs choked her body and her shoulders shook.

"Miss Annalise?"

Annalise hadn't heard a knock at the door. When she turned her face, she saw Jinny standing in the doorway. "Do you want that I should bring supper to your room?"

Supper sounded as appetizing as eating a dirt clod, even if it was one of Henrietta's delicious meals. "Yes. Thank you, Jinny."

Jinny softly closed the door behind her. Taking a risk that could get her beaten or worse, Jinny sat on the edge of the bed and patted Annalise's arm. "I'm sorry, Miss Annalise."

Annalise leaned her head on Jinny's shoulder and Jinny wrapped a thin arm around her. "Now, now. Let those tears fall."

"I'm so sorry, Jinny."

"For what?"

"Tandey was beaten because of me. Because of my choice to go for a ride. I'm so sorry."

"Now, now. Don't fret. You've been a good mistress. Always caring for us and looking out for us from the time your parents done owned us. It wasn't your fault none, but the master's."

"Thank you, Jinny, but I am sorry and I will make it up to both of you someday."

Annalise made sure her voice was lowered. If Aunt Lavinia heard her speaking to Jinny, there was no telling what Uncle Phineas would do to Jinny. "Matthias doesn't trust me," she croaked in a hoarse whisper, forgetting for a moment that Jinny had no idea who Matthias was. "Maybe I should just marry that hideous Dale Hiram."

"Don't you dare do such a thing," Jinny gasped, her big brown eyes growing even larger with concern. "That man is horrid, and you and I both done know it."

"But if Matthias doesn't trust me..."

"Your sorrow is speaking for you. You and I both know you have feelings for Matthias, just the same as I have feelings for Tandey. Everyone makes mistakes, and maybe his words just didn't come out right is all. I don't know about the situation none, but I'm sure this Matthias fellow cares for you."

"You're right, Jinny. I need to show him grace. He's carrying a heavy burden right now. It's just hard not to be doleful after all that's happened today."

"I done saw your aunt's wrath poured out on you." Jinny patted Annalise's shoulder. "Now you just cry some good tears because then you'll have to put on a happy face so as your aunt doesn't suspect you all the more."

Annalise sighed. "You're right. Whatever would I do without you? Remember those days back at our other home? We would play with our dolls and have such jubilant times."

"Oh, I remember them days." A smile lit Jinny's sweet face.

"It was the most wonderful thing having a friend the same age."

"Yes, it was."

"Did you ever feel scared for your life at our old home, Jinny?"

"Never, not once. I did miss my mama and papa like you do now, but your folks, they took good care of me and treated me well. Almost like I wasn't owned at all."

"Thank you for being a good friend."

"I'm always here for you, Miss Annalise. You know that. Times is tough, but the Lord, He watches over us and He has a plan. A mighty good plan for His children."

Guilt overwhelmed Annalise. Jinny's life had taken a turn for the worse after Mother and Father passed. She'd been beaten and worse at the hands of Uncle Phineas and his slave overseers. "I have no right to complain after all you've been through."

"Pain is pain. We both suffered enough of it for sure. Don't you apologize none for being sad. Didn't your mama say that tears are God's way of washing all that sadness away and making way for a smile?"

"She did indeed. Jinny, do you know what we are?"

"In a whole heap of trouble if your aunt hears us talking?"

"That too. But we are sisters in the Lord."

"Yes we are, and we be praying for each other."

"Yes, and someday, somehow, I'm going to see to it that you and Tandey are freed."

CHAPTER FIFTEEN

MATTHIAS STOOD BEHIND THE pulpit ready to preach the sermon. He scanned the crowd. Would Annalise be there after his accusatory words? Matthias swallowed hard. He never should have expressed that concern. Since he had come to know her, Matthias had realized how different she was from his first assumptions about her. He *knew* Annalise would do nothing to compromise the Faith Train, whether intentional or accidental. He knew that with every fiber of his being. Just like he knew that he was falling in love with the beautiful woman with a heart for others.

Lord, please give me the opportunity to apologize.

Matthias again scanned the rows of pews. No sign of Annalise. Had she been apprehended by her uncle? Worry wormed its way into his heart.

Casting all your care upon him; for he careth for you. The verse entered Matthias's mind and propelled him to remember the sin of worry and how it had grasped so fiercely onto him, not only in the situation with the freeing of the slaves, but also throughout his life. Wasn't that the topic he was preaching on this very day? Not to worry? Not to fret? Not to fear? But to cast all of his cares on the Lord? That the Lord would sustain him?

The last thing Matthias desired was to be a hypocrite. He had prayed time and time again that the Lord would free him from the bondage of worry and fear. For how could a man of the cloth doubt that his precious Savior would protect him? And a man of the cloth couldn't preach about it when he didn't himself live it.

Matthias shoved the thoughts of guilt aside. He hadn't slept much as of late, between his concern for Annalise, his regret over the insinuations he had made to her, and the prospect of preaching on a sermon that would likely help him more than it would help his congregation.

One of the elders cleared his throat, catching Matthias off-guard, and he brought his mind to the present. His congregation stared at him expectantly, awaiting his wisdom from the Word. Matthias wouldn't fail them.

Lord, please give me the words You wish for me to speak. Help me to digest and apply each word of truth from Your Bible that I am about to quote. Free me from the fears and worries that overtake my mind. And, Father, please give me the opportunity to apologize and reconcile with Annalise.

"Good morning. Let's open with a word of prayer."

After the opening prayer, the singing of several hymns, and the announcements, Matthias again took his place behind the pulpit. That's when he saw Annalise, walking down the aisle toward her newfound place beside Betsy and Adam.

Thank You, Lord.

His eyes connected with hers and she looked away. *Lord, another chance with her. Please?*

Matthias set aside the turmoil roiling inside him about his conversation with Annalise and addressed the congregation with a renewed sense of peace.

Annalise had been drawn in by Matthias's sermon. Oh, she was always captivated by the words of the gifted young man she had grown so fond of in recent months, but this time something about him was different. Almost as if the words Matthias spoke were directed toward something more personal.

She hadn't slept well over the past two nights, going over and what Matthias had said and what he really must think of her. Annalise wished she could request that he do a sermon on dwelling on a topic repeatedly. She needed advice when it came to that trap she found herself in whenever something upsetting, frightening, or irritating happened.

Their eyes connected several times throughout the church service, eyes that she longed to gaze into without interruption. She admired Matthias and his tenderness and compassion toward others.

Annalise pulled her mind back to the service. She ought not think about such things of a man who wasn't courting her, and especially in church. Annalise offered a prayer seeking the Lord's forgiveness.

And, Lord, would you please allow Matthias and I reconcile?

When the service concluded, Matthias walked toward her. "Annalise?"

"Hello, Matthias."

"Could we speak after the other parishioners have left?"

Annalise nodded. She wanted nothing more.

It took some time for Matthias to offer goodbyes to the faithful members of his church. In the meantime, Annalise spoke to the people who had embraced her when she first arrived, even though she was different from them. Some congregants still eyed her with suspicion, but for the most part, she had been accepted because each person in the church had one important thing in common: their love for Christ.

"Thank you for waiting, Annalise."

Her heart leapt at his voice. Feelings of elation filled her when in his presence. Were she to someday marry him...

I can no more marry Matthias than turn Uncle Phineas into a decent man. Besides, how can I even begin to think of marriage when we are not courting? And wasn't I irritated and saddened about Matthias's words just this morning? The word *capricious* came to Annalise's mind and she almost giggled at the description of herself.

"Annalise..." Matthias reached to place a hand on her arm.

Something akin to butterflies zipped up her arm. "Yes?"

"I am so sorry. Please forgive me for my accusations. I sometimes become so consumed in worry about the Faith Train failing that I forget God is in control. I know I upset you with my words, and I pray you will give me a chance to make amends."

"I forgive you, Matthias. You must understand that I would never, ever do anything intentional, accidental, or otherwise to compromise the Faith Train. I have too much vested in it myself, and I care deeply for those we assist. I have been extra cautious at all times of Uncle Phineas's watchful eye."

His hand slipped from her arm to brush her fingertips before returning to his side. "I know that, Annalise. I do. I can't tell you what a huge benefit you have been to the organization. We would not have been able to accomplish as much without your help. And with your sacrifice -—and I'm certain it was a sacrifice—to come and warn me about the slave bait your uncle is planning, there is no way I can thank you adequately. You may have saved my life and the lives of countless others with that act of bravery."

Matthias's eyes almost seemed misty—something one wouldn't expect from a man so masculine and seemingly tough when moving slaves through the network.

But Matthias had a tender side. A side that Annalise was quickly growing to love.

They spoke in hushed tones, for even the church could have someone listening who was set to thwart their plans. "Please promise me, Matthias, that you won't give in to the slave that Uncle Phineas sends."

"But how will I know who he is? Slaves approach me weekly with the code, expecting my assistance—our assistance—in securing their freedom. How will I know which one is false?"

"They have a slave chosen just for this purpose." Annalise wished she could recall the name of the slave. "But you are right, it will be difficult to know. Sheriff Bleyer and the others know of your code with the tugging at your right ear."

"They do?"

"Yes."

Matthias shook his head. "Then we must develop a new code."

"Yes. But until then, potential runaways will be using that code. You mustn't assist any slaves for the next few weeks until I can glean further information from Uncle Phineas and his friends."

"A few weeks is a long time to refuse help to someone. Especially those who are innocent."

"I agree, but it must be done. You know that."

Matthias appeared reluctant.

Lord, please help him to see.

"You are correct, Annalise. This one error could stop our entire mission. As it is, we are sending a telegram tomorrow to others in the network that we are delaying sending more slaves for the next few weeks. I don't like it, but it's something we must do. Betsy, Adam, the others, and I spoke of it last night.

"We can again offer our assistance once Uncle Phineas has given up on his plan."

"But will he ever abandon his plan?"

Annalise doubted it. "Likely not. But in the meantime, as you say, we can develop other methods of spreading the word about how help can be accessed for those in slavery."

"Yes."

"Because, Matthias, I couldn't endure it if something happened to you. Uncle Phineas is bent on hanging you, whether a judge finds you guilty or not. And a judge would, given Uncle Phineas's influence."

"I'm not about to allow myself to be hanged. I have too much to live for."

They stood for a moment, their eyes and hearts connected in this moment of time. Would they ever find the freedom to express their feelings toward each other? Two people from different social classes. Annalise with strong restrictions upon her life by her nefarious uncle. How could they ever hope to court, let alone marry?

And did Matthias even feel the same way she did? Annalise pushed the thought aside. There was another pressing matter.

"Matthias, when Uncle Phineas relents somewhat, promise me one thing?"

"Anything."

"Promise me we will do all we can to help Jinny and Tandey escape."

"I promise I will do everything in my power."

If the two were allowed to escape, perhaps they could marry as they had dreamed for some time. Something most folks took for granted.

Matthias couldn't take his eyes from her. Not only was the woman before him lovely, kind, spirited, and brave, but she was also a woman of forgiveness.

And the one who had captured his heart long before even he knew it.

"If only you didn't have an Uncle Phineas, I would ask to take you on a Sunday drive."

The corners of Annalise's mouth turned up in the pleasing smile Matthias had grown to admire. "It just so happens that Uncle Phineas and Aunt Lavinia are in Knoxville until tomorrow. A Sunday drive would be most delightful."

Chapter Sixteen

SPENDING TIME WITH MATTHIAS was nothing short of a dream come true. Aunt Lavinia and Uncle Phineas so rarely left town that when they had announced their trip to Knoxville, Annalise feared she hadn't heard correctly.

Yet, here she was in a buggy that Matthias had rented from the livery, traveling down the road toward a charming picnic spot he had picked out just for them. While Annalise knew the time with Matthias would be short since there was no telling when her aunt and uncle would really return and no telling who might see them, she planned to make the most of every moment.

"This is a lovely spot, Matthias."

The location for the picnic was a plush spot near a river. "I had to have somewhere special to take someone special."

Had it been only two days ago that Annalise doubted her feelings for Matthias? Only two days ago that she had given thought to marrying Dale Hiram? *Thank You, Lord, for reconciliation.*

Matthias lifted her from the buggy. Setting her down, he held her at the waist, his eyes looking into hers. "Annalise..."

Would he kiss her? She hoped so! Was it scandalous that she hoped for that? They stood for what seemed like a lengthy time gazing into each other's eyes. Matthias reached up with one hand and touched her cheek. "You're beautiful."

Annalise attempted to find words to respond, but couldn't. Any response remained stuck in her throat. He leaned toward her, his lips pressing against her forehead and his arms finding their way around her waist once again. Annalise closed her eyes and relished the moment, feeling safe enfolded in the strong arms of the man she had come to care for. He smelled like a combination of pine trees and soap. Her pulse quickened and she wondered if Matthias could hear her heartbeat.

Annalise could remain here forever.

Matthias whispered in her ear. "Shall we have our picnic?"

She leaned back and stared up at him. "We shall."

He smiled the crooked smile that showed all the more the dimple in his chin. "I'll retrieve the basket."

With the basket of food that Betsy had prepared in one hand, Matthias reached for Annalise's hand with the other and led her to a spot by the river. "What a blessing to have your aunt and uncle out of town."

"Indeed. Although who knows how long they will be gone."

"We will make the most, then, of the time we are given." They said grace before eating the fried chicken Betsy had prepared.

"It's a frightening time with all that's going on."

"Yes, but let's not speak of that right now. Instead, let's speak of another pressing matter."

"Another one?" Wasn't all they had experienced enough?

"Yes, the pressing matter of falling in love with a beautiful woman named Annalise Van Houten."

Of all the things Annalise thought Matthias would say, she hadn't figured he would say that. Had she heard him correctly? "I beg your pardon?"

"I know you are accustomed to finery. I can't offer you that. I've been a reverend and, before that, a farmer. I don't have much to offer you. I don't even own a home. I do, however, own a fine horse." His mouth quirked to one side.

"I don't care if you don't own a fine home, Matthias."

"Someday—and it's looking like it might be sooner than I had expected—I will be leaving Ridge Gap. I will continue to do the work that the Lord has called me to—that of preaching and helping the slaves. Neither calling will amass a small fortune with which to support a wife and family."

"The Lord's work offers rewards much more important than money and possessions. A wise reverend once preached on that very topic."

Matthias grinned. "So you were listening."

"You didn't think I'd dare sleep through your sermons?"

"There was that one time when it appeared your head was bobbing, and I figured you to be nearly asleep."

"Well, if I remember correctly, that was a sermon on the Book of Numbers."

Matthias chuckled, a deep, throaty laugh that Annalise realized she didn't want to go without hearing for even one day.

He stopped and his face took on a serious demeanor. He reached for her hands and held them in his. "Annalise, life with me won't be easy. It will be full of worry at times and the type of adventure that can cause stomach upsets."

"Stomach upsets? Matthias, you are a romantic at heart. I know life with you won't be easy. You are making a difference in the lives of countless people. Every day you undertake assignments, most of which I am unaware of."

"It is for your safety and for the safety of the Faith Train that we don't know the exact details, nor the others involved in the undertakings of freeing the slaves."

Such secrecy was necessary should one of them be caught and questioned. What one didn't know, one couldn't share.

"Anyhow, I guess what I'm failing miserably at trying to say is that I wish to court you and, Lord willing, marry you someday." He paused. "May I court you?"

"Yes, Matthias, yes, you may."

"I can't exactly ask your uncle for his blessing or permission, and I know he intends you to marry Dale Hiram."

"I'll not marry Dale Hiram. Ever." *Yet, two days ago, you believed that to be your only option.* Annalise pushed the rebuke aside.

"I've spent time with the Lord seeking His guidance as to whether courting in secret is acceptable. If you'll have me, I'd like to make you my wife. Although, as I said, I can't offer you anything."

"You can offer me the most important things, Matthias. Your love and devotion."

"You will have both of those. You'll also have my orneriness at times."

"And you shall have mine. Along with a bit of stubbornness thrown in for good measure."

They laughed again, causing Annalise to forget that she must return to her life in short order.

"So it doesn't bother you I don't have much? That we may have to live in a meager log cabin?"

"Will I be with you?"

"Yes."

"Then a meager log cabin will do just fine. Right now, I am prisoner in the home of Aunt Lavinia and Uncle Phineas. I would prefer living in a shack in freedom than living in a mansion in bondage. Unfortunately, I suspect my aunt and uncle have squandered my inheritance, so I may have nothing to offer either. We could have used that money for so much good."

"I never loved you for your inheritance, Annalise. I fell in love with you for your benevolent heart and your willingness to sacrifice yourself for another. And, of course, your beauty." He grinned.

"I am content just to have the honor of being your wife."

"You've made me a happy man." Matthias leaned forward. "May I kiss you?"

Before Annalise could answer, Matthias had leaned forward. Their newfound love was sealed when his lips found hers in a combination of gentleness and passion.

CHAPTER SEVENTEEN

IF ONLY ALL OF her life could be as peaceful as the Sunday and Monday that Aunt Lavinia and Uncle Phineas were in Knoxville. But it was not to remain so. On Tuesday, not only did they return, but Aunt Lavinia presented Annalise with some disturbing news.

"Dale Hiram is to be our guest tonight. You will do your utmost to be pleasant and worthy of his affections."

If only Annalise could escape the clutches of her aunt and uncle. Her mind continued to retreat to the delightful time she had spent with Matthias during their picnic. What would it be like to spend every waking moment with the man of her affections? What would it be like to make a life with him, rather than the life she was living against her will?

She might never know.

Dale Hiram arrived at the Thorn household promptly at seven. Annalise sat in the front parlor awkwardly facing him as he attempted idle chit-chat with her. His leering gaze and arrogant attitude induced nausea. His harsh, darkened eyes pierced through her without blinking, and his jaw was set firm in his motionless face. Mr. Hiram locked into Annalise's shifting gaze, seemingly willing her to accede to his overt domination. Barely taller than Annalise, he exuded an air of superiority.

"Mr. Hiram, as you know, has one of the largest plantations in the area. You would do well to appreciate that he has chosen you as the future Mrs. Hiram," gloated Aunt Lavinia.

The future Mrs. Hiram? The thought caused Annalise's chest to constrict and her breathing to become labored. *Never!*

Mr. Hiram puffed out his chest. "I intend to expand my plantation to the border of Father's land. I recently purchased the acreage on the north side."

And I should find this impressive? I'm being married off to the first bidder since I no longer have an inheritance and nothing left to offer a greedy aunt and uncle.

"We feel that, based on current circumstances, it would be in the best interests of everyone involved for you to begin courtship with Mr. Hiram posthaste. As Mr. Hiram and I have discussed, your wedding shall commence as soon as we are able to arrange it."

As soon as they were able to arrange it? "This is highly unconventional." Annalise's voice shook.

"While it is short notice and much needs to be done before the wedding, I am confident that between Mr. Hiram's mother, myself, and the ladies in our society, such a feat can be achieved without much difficulty."

"With all due respect, shouldn't there be a longer courtship period? After all, Mr. Hiram and I barely know each other."

A slight flicker in Mr. Hiram's sinister glare told Annalise that he was not happy with her suggestion. His words confirmed it. "Now, now, Miss Van Houten. Is a long engagement necessary? Your family and my family are of equal social standing. Would this not make for a match that would combine affluence in the most beneficial manner?"

But I am betrothed to another, a man I love. Annalise, however, couldn't mention this. Neither her aunt nor her uncle would ever find Matthias of suitable social standing to court, much less, marry her. *Lord, please, I beseech Thee to assist me in this most horrific matter. Show me a way to escape.*

"Have you nothing to say in response to Mr. Hiram's statement?" Uncle Phineas asked, daring her to respond.

"I simply feel that we should have a longer courtship." *Thereby giving me ample time to escape the clutches of this bondage.*

Uncle Phineas pounded his fist on the table beside the overstuffed chair on which he sat. "Nonsense! I'll not hear of it. The joining of the Thorn and Hiram families will suit us all quite well."

"But I am a Van Houten." The words escaped Annalise's lips before she could restrain them.

Uncle Phineas gritted his teeth, his red face rivaling Aunt Lavinia's rose bushes. "You will do as we say and you will be grateful for the opportunity, Annalise."

"But—"

"Perhaps for her squabbling, we should hasten the wedding all the more," suggested Aunt Lavinia, a malevolent smirk lining her hateful face.

"Aunt Lavinia, please."

"Not to worry, *my dear*. Any objections, Mr. Hiram?"

"No objections at all, Mrs. Thorn. The sooner I make Annalise my wife, the better for everyone."

The tears fell and she could not stop them. She wished she could retreat to her room, but knew better than to leave the presence of her menacing relatives. Instead, she prayed fervently and when she finished, she woolgathered for the remainder of the conversation between her uncle and Dale Hiram.

When she excused herself to her room after supper, she heard the words of her future husband loud and clear. "Now that we have that matter settled, Phineas, lets rid ourselves of Reverend Sorenson."

CHAPTER EIGHTEEN

Matthias walked up the boardwalk after his visit to the livery. He had accomplished much on this Tuesday, despite his mind being elsewhere.

On a comely woman with sparkling eyes, for instance.

He couldn't stop thinking about Annalise and how they had spoken of courtship and someday marriage. He couldn't stop thanking the Lord that Annalise had given him a second chance after his careless words. If only he had more to offer the woman who had stolen a place in his heart.

"Love and devotion are the most important things you can give someone," Bets had declared when he'd told her Annalise had accepted his courtship. "The two of you will be able to serve the Lord even more so together than individually. You have found your true helpmate, Matthias."

Whistling, Matthias thought of how he had successfully sent the telegram to his parents in Ohio that the "parcel" he was sending would be the last for some time.

He hadn't mentioned his plans to leave and move to Ohio in the coming month. That was not something he could send in a telegram. Not with the nosy postal clerk honing in on every word.

Besides, Matthias needed to address his congregation and tell them he had been called to another flock. Thankfully, there were several trusted individuals in the church who would carry on the role of the Faith Train in Ridge Gap after he, Adam, and Betsy left.

Gratitude engulfed him that Thorn and Bleyer did not suspect the other Faith Train members.

He reminded himself he had to discuss his plans with Annalise and reassure her that he would return for her next spring.

Matthias had secured a wagon for today's load of "potatoes." He had managed to get Tandey and Jinny off the plantation, but the delivery was risky, especially given Mr. Thorn's preoccupation with Matthias's supposed role in the Faith Train. He had worried most of the night, but the Lord continued to help Matthias overcome his fears daily.

The Lord Almighty would deliver both Tandey and Jinny to their freedom.

Matthias had to believe that. Just as he had to believe that the Lord would protect him, Annalise, Betsy, and Adam.

A slave ambled behind his owner, carrying a weighty sack of flour. A master Matthias did not recognize. The slave tugged on his ear, and Matthias did a double-take.

Another person seeking freedom whom Matthias was called to assist.

He lingered by the mercantile, eyeing the slave and awaiting a moment of time to confront him.

Within minutes, the slave had turned and headed back toward the mercantile, presumably for a second load. Matthias purposely ran into him. "Watch where you are going," he said.

"Sir, can you help me escape?" the slave asked, his voice more of a hiss.

Something indiscernible in the slave's eyes caught Matthias off-guard. A jolt sent warnings through him.

But why? Never before had warning signals presented themselves in such an odd manner. Or at all, for that matter.

"Sir, can you?" The slave took a rapid glance back toward his master, then at Matthias, then back at his master once again. A shifty demeanor radiated from him, as the slave transferred his weight from one foot to the other.

Was he concerned his master would inquire why the slave had so brazenly confronted Matthias in public?

Matthias stared at the man. He should say "yes" and give the man hope of freedom. While Matthias didn't know any of the conductors on the railroad between here and "The Promised Land", he did know that once the man reached Ohio, Matthias's parents would be eager to help him continue his journey to Canada.

"Uh..." Matthias had never been speechless before when asked this question. Why was this time different?

How many slaves had he assisted? At least twenty-five, counting Tandey and Jinny, and that was just in the past year. Matthias took in his surroundings and noticed that the master had not been waiting for the slave, nor insistent upon his quick return.

Something wasn't right.

"Please promise me, Matthias, that you won't give in to the slave that Uncle Phineas sends."

"Sir, ain't you gonna help me?" the slave's voice almost came out as a sneer.

Annalise's words pierced Matthias's mind, almost as if they were spoken aloud.

Was this the slave that Phineas Thorn had sent? How would Matthias know for sure?

"Reverend Sorenson!" Mrs. Knapp's voice sounded from across the street. Her hand waved frantically in Matthias's direction. "Oh, Reverend Sorenson! May I have a moment of your time?"

Lord, are You trying to tell me something?

Matthias cleared his throat. "I'm sorry, but I don't assist slaves in running away. You'd best get back to work or I will tell your master." He held the man's gaze.

The man quirked an eyebrow, as if pondering whether to believe Matthias's words. "Yes, sir," he finally said, his lips tightened and curled inward.

"Reverend Sorenson, I'm so glad I caught up with you." Mrs. Knapp's round face loomed as she bustled near him. "Did you not hear my calling?" She knit her thick eyebrows together.

Oh, Matthias had heard her all right. For Mrs. Knapp might easily have been the tool the Lord used in saving many lives that day.

Before the recent turn of events, Annalise never would have imagined herself to be a busybody who eavesdropped on the conversations of others. But it had become necessary.

She rounded the corner of the parlor where Aunt Lavinia and Uncle Phineas sat on overstuffed chairs. The pungent odor of Uncle Phineas's cigar swirled toward her. Add that to the list of things she wouldn't miss when she left.

"Reverend Sorenson didn't fall for our plan with the slave, so the men and I are talking about taking further steps. That man needs to be stopped." Uncle Phineas paused. "While I cannot prove it, I have every reason to believe that he is why two more of our slaves have gone missing."

"I am sure you are right about him, Phineas. If you and the menfolk decided to take extreme measures, it wouldn't be the first time blood has been shed upon your direct order."

Annalise sucked in a deep breath. Were Uncle Phineas and his cronies planning to take Matthias's life? *No, Father, please don't allow that to happen!*

Uncle Phineas chuckled, a low, rolling, thunderous laugh that caused chills to ripple up Annalise's spine. "I am quite cunning, if I do say so myself."

"Indeed."

"On a more serious note, if we continue to lose slaves, we will no longer have a plantation. I cannot afford to keep purchasing new ones to replace those the good reverend has helped to escape. We have already used all of the money Annalise's parents left when they died."

Aunt Lavinia laughed a high-pitched cackle. Annalise squeezed her eyes shut. Her aunt and uncle had wasted all of her family's fortune? That quickly? Without her knowledge? While Annalise had suspected the loss of her inheritance, this confirmed the greed of her aunt and uncle.

"When do you plan to execute your scheme against the reverend?"

"Next week. Sheriff Bleyer, Luther, and I discussed some of the details at Luther's home last night."

Annalise heard Aunt Lavinia clap her hands. "Splendid! After that, we will plan the wedding for Annalise. The sooner we are rid of her, the better. Dale will put that impertinent young woman in her place."

She had to leave the life she knew. Her aunt and uncle's plan to fatally harm Matthias, their plot of forcing Annalise to marry Dale Hiram, and the loss of Annalise's inheritance confirmed her decision. There was only one thing to do.

Beg Matthias to take her with him when he left Ridge Gap.

The second Nehemiah stopped the carriage, Annalise leapt from it, not waiting for the slave's assistance. She had to catch Matthias before services started.

He sat in the front pew, likely praying, as he always did before delivering the sermon. "Matthias!" her voice sounded breathless. Only a matter of minutes remained before members of the congregation arrived.

"Annalise, so nice to see you." Matthias unfolded his hands and stood. He took a step toward her. "What's wrong?"

"Matthias, you have to take me with you when you and the others leave. Please."

"What happened?"

She took a deep breath and began to speak, her words sounding jumbled even to her own ears.

"Annalise, please slow down." He gently reached for her upper arms, as a look of concern spread across his handsome face.

Where should she start? And with so few moments of privacy? "Matthias..." she lowered her voice. "I am so thankful my uncle's first plan did not work. But Uncle Phineas, Sheriff Bleyer, and the others are not going to stop. They want to destroy the Faith Train, and everyone involved, especially you."

"Annalise—"

She shook her head and put a soft finger to his lips. "Please hear my words. They are planning to take your life."

A look of alarm crossed over Matthias's face and Annalise fought the bile that rose in her throat. "This will happen next week."

"We plan to leave in two days."

"Good." She closed her eyes and offered another quick prayer heavenward. "Take me with you," she begged. "Please. By the time you return for me, my marriage to Dale Hiram will have already commenced."

Matthias shook his head and a look of determination lined his face. "I will never allow them to marry you off to Dale Hiram. I don't want to lose you."

"Then please take me with you."

Matthias removed his hands from her arms. "It will be dangerous taking you from the Thorn Plantation."

"You recently assisted Jinny and Tandy from that very place." She jutted her chin out. She must get away from her aunt and uncle at any cost.

A sparkle lit his eyes and he smiled. "Why do I think I can ever win a battle with you?" He placed a kiss on her forehead. "Annalise, we will take you with us, but I must make one request: that you will find me fitting to be your husband."

"Are you proposing?"

"What better place than in the Lord's house?"

Annalise giggled, a laugh that felt good after all the trepidation she had experienced. "My answer is 'yes'."

"That's the answer I was hoping for." Matthias paused, looking at the door as if expecting a parishioner to walk through it at any moment. "I love you, Annalise."

"I love you, too." And she did, with every part of her being.

"After church, we will discuss the plans for your escape." His words momentarily settled her fears.

Matthias hadn't been looking forward to bidding his congregation farewell. He would miss the fine folks of Ridge Gap and this little church that had been his place to serve the Lord for such a short time.

"It is with mixed feelings that I must say goodbye to this congregation. Some of you have known of my plans before now, while this is the first time others of you have heard this news." He paused and regarded the faces of the people of whom he had grown so fond.

"The Lord has called me to another place to serve Him. The life of a reverend is never dull when we have absolutely surrendered to His will. However, I would not have it any other way."

Sniffles erupted and Matthias found he was having a difficult time containing his own feelings. "Until a permanent replacement is found, Mr. Lawton will lead the church."

His eyes then met Annalise's gaze.

He loved her.

And soon, Lord willing, they would begin their new lives together in Ohio.

"Annalise, are you coming in for the evening?" Aunt Lavinia poked her head out the door where Annalise sat on the veranda in a rocking chair.

"Soon, Aunt Lavinia, soon. For now, I am taking a moment to escape the heat of the house."

Aunt Lavinia narrowed her eyes. Would she accept Annalise's flimsy excuse? "Very well. But neither your Uncle Phineas nor I will wait up to accommodate your ridiculous antics of sitting outside until the wee hours of the night."

Wee hours was correct. If that's what it took to proceed with her plan, then that was what Annalise would do. "Not to worry. I will be in soon."

Without so much as a kindly farewell, Aunt Lavinia stepped back into the house, leaving Annalise to her thoughts.

And to the three very long hours that awaited her.

In the distance, she could hear singing, likely from some slaves, as they finished their night time chores. A whiff of something cooking reached her and Annalise's stomach growled. Good thing she had packed a sandwich in her carpetbag.

She glanced to where she had hidden the only items she would be taking with her to her new life. From an exhaustive supply of fancy dresses to three meager ones, Annalise's life was about to change.

For the better.

She begged the night to come faster, as she slowly rocked in the chair. Every few minutes, Annalise checked the pocket watch she held in her lap. She mustn't be late to meet Matthias and the others.

Sometime later, all of the lanterns in the house and elsewhere grew dim. The only sound was the snoring of Mr. Talon.

Mr. Talon.

The hideous man Uncle Phineas had hired three days ago to provide surveillance over the plantation at night-fall.

That man unsettled her. From his ogling when Uncle Phineas first introduced them to his spiteful words toward the slaves, Annalise knew Mr. Talon was not a man she wanted to cross paths with. His name fit him well as his face had the appearance of a pinched bird beak. He reminded Annalise of a bird of prey settling his eerie gaze on his victim.

He was somewhere near the barn. The man would take no mercy on her life if he found her sneaking off into the night during his watch.

Lord, please, please be with me as I go forward with this plan. Let it be successful.

At the proper time, Annalise stood, reached for her carpetbag, then slowly meandered down the steps of the veranda. Constantly looking to and fro, she tiptoed past the barn, where she eyed Mr. Talon lying on the ground.

Obnoxious wheezing sounds came from his open mouth, and a bottle of whiskey sat beside his right hand. A rifle lay across his chest.

She almost turned back to the house.

No, I must keep going. I must. For if she didn't, Annalise would be married to Dale Hiram and forever be his prisoner.

And a life without Matthias was a life she didn't want to live.

Out of the eyesight of Mr. Talon, Annalise took to a run. She must only make it to the gate at the edge of the plantation where Matthias and the others would meet her. It wasn't that far. Not really.

Why then, did it feel as though it was an eternity from the house to the gate? She willed her breath to quiet. Her heart rumbled in her chest and her carpetbag slid off her elbow and clunked against her wrist. Clasping it in her hand, Annalise increased her speed.

A noise startled her. Mr. Talon? Could he have discovered her presence?

She glanced behind her and thought she saw something. Or someone. Had Aunt Lavinia or Uncle Phineas realized she hadn't returned to the house?

A thought rammed through her mind. Was this how the slaves felt as they escaped?

For she didn't doubt for a moment that her life would be at risk if she were caught.

Ahead was the gate. Just a few more steps...Once she was in the wagon, a friend of Matthias's would take them to the next town where they would stay the night before embarking on their journey to Ohio.

Would they make it there safely?

As Annalise crossed over from one side of the gate to the other, she nearly collapsed from both exhaustion and gratitude.

Strong arms lifted her and carried her to the awaiting wagon. "You're safe now, Annalise," Matthias whispered.

Epilogue

THINGS HAD BEEN A flurry of excitement over the past two months. After Annalise and Matthias had traveled to their new home in Ohio, Matthias, with the assistance of so many others in the Faith Train network, had helped Tandey and Jinny complete their journey to freedom. And Annalise could finally put her heart at rest knowing that her dear friends were safe.

Matthias squeezed her hand, and Annalise gazed up at the man she had married just one short week ago.

How I love him!

For now, Annalise and Matthias would reside in a humble cabin about a mile from Matthias's parents, who also had a position in the Faith Train. Betsy and Adam resided not far from them.

Annalise and Matthias had joined not only in matrimony, but also in a role the Lord had placed them in aiding slaves in reaching freedom.

Only He knew what was planned for them at the next juncture.

When Matthias leaned in to plant a passionate kiss on Annalise's waiting lips, she knew one thing to be true. She had found freedom.

Author's Note

When I discovered I would be originally writing this story for a Barbour Publishing Collection, I was ecstatic. I immediately began researching the Underground Railroad and was humbled by all of the people who put their lives at jeopardy to free those in slavery.

From harboring them, to moving them along the network, to forming rescue operations, to feeding and clothing them, these brave men and woman made a difference for countless individuals. Many of those involved in freeing slaves were pastors, hence my inspiration for Matthias Sorenson.

The Faith Train, the term used in *Freedom's Flight*, is of my own imagination, but was intended to operate much as the Underground Railroad did.

My end goal was, of course, a happy ending. (I *only* write books with happy endings). But also to have a couple who worked together on this mission. Betsy and Adam, Matthias's parents, and later Matthias and Annalise, would all fit this category. My inspiration for such a couple was Levi and Catherine Coffin.

As with all books, I was sad to see this one end. As it began as a Barbour Collection novella, word count was critical, and I knew my main focus would be securing the freedom of Annalise, Tandey, and Jinny. As a writer, ideas percolate in my mind on a continual basis (most oftentimes when I should be sleeping!) and I have thought of a possible idea for a sequel. Stay tuned.

ACKNOWLEDGMENTS

To my family. I can never thank you enough for your encouragement, support, and patience as I put words to paper. I'm so grateful for you.

To my Penny's Peeps Street Team. Thank you for spreading the word about my books. I appreciate your support!

To my readers. May God bless and guide you as you grow in your walk with Him.

And, most importantly, thank you to my Lord and Savior, Jesus Christ. It is my deepest desire to glorify You with my writing and help bring others to a knowledge of Your saving grace.

ABOUT THE AUTHOR

Penny Zeller is known for her heartfelt stories of faith and her passion to impact lives for Christ through fiction. While she has had a love for writing since childhood, she began her adult writing career penning articles for national and regional publications on a wide variety of topics. Today, Penny is the author of over a dozen books. She is also a homeschool mom and a fitness instructor.

When Penny is not dreaming up new characters, she enjoys spending time with her husband and two daughters, camping, hiking, canoeing, reading, running, cycling, gardening, and playing volleyball.

She is represented by Tamela Hancock Murray of the Steve Laube Agency and loves to hear from her readers at her website and her blog, *random thoughts from a day in the life of a wife, mom, and author*, at .

Social Media Links: https://linktr.ee/pennyzeller

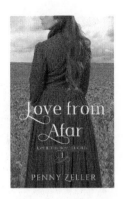

*What happens when two little sisters become
self-appointed matchmakers?*

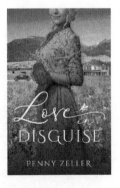

*Who knew concealing one's identity
could be so disastrous?*

Take a glimpse into where it all began with Lydie and Solomon's story in this tender tale that reminds us that God can and does use willing hearts for His purposes.

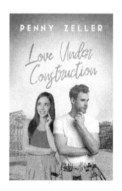

She builds websites. He builds houses. Together, can they build a family for two orphans?

Made in the USA
Columbia, SC
15 October 2022